Born in Brighton, musician ⟨...⟩ as composer and sound designer ⟨...⟩ and television. He has also released a number of solo albums on labels such as Third Kind, Spun Out Of Control and Modern Aviation.

He lives in Switzerland with his wife and two children.

ALSO BY RUPERT LALLY:

Solid State Memories

Backwater

RUPERT LALLY

TEENAGE WILDLIFE

This paperback edition published 2023
Text ©2023 Rupert Lally

ISBN: 9798397146029
Imprint: Independently published

The right of Rupert Lally to be identified as the author of this work has been asserted by him in accordance with the Copyright, Designs and Patents Act 1988

All Rights reserved. No part of this publication may be reproduced, stored in a retrieval system, or transmitted, in any form, or by any means (electronic, mechanical, photocopying, recording or otherwise) without the prior written permission of the author.

This book is sold subject to the condition that it shall not, by way of trade or otherwise, be lent, hired out, or otherwise circulated without the publisher's prior consent in any form of binding or cover other than that in which it is published and without a similar condition including this condition being imposed on the subsequent publisher.

TEENAGE WILDLIFE

Author's Note

This novel contains several instances of homophobic slurs which would be unacceptable today, but were in common usage in 1987. I hope readers will accept their inclusion for the sake of historical accuracy.

R.L.

I hope you don't mind if I record these sessions? It's just for my own reference, later on, you understand? Anything you say here remains strictly confidential.

No, that's fine. I mean, I don't mind.

Good. So, I'd like to start by thanking you for your account of what occurred. There were some aspects that troubled me, however.

In terms of what I described, you mean?

It's more how you chose to describe them.

I tried to be as honest as I could.

Yes and some parts are extremely detailed, but can you not see that there might have been an alternative way of describing the events, that would have made more sense?

I just tried to write it all down in a way that seemed logical.

I see. Perhaps, you wouldn't mind just going through it again, for me.

The whole thing?

Yes please. Just take me through it all, once more, in your own words.

1: BLUE MONDAY

It must have been a Monday. It felt like a Monday and looking back I'm sure I had that typical sense of lethargy that I'd always associated with Mondays when I was at school. For some reason, since I'd started secondary school, I'd come to dread Mondays. The feeling began to creep in midway through Sunday afternoon, generally when I was finally forced to get on with whatever homework I'd put off since coming home on Friday.

In essence it was same reaction that I had at the end of every school holiday, in microcosm. At their start, both weekends and holidays seemed to stretch off into the distance, filled with the promise of longer lie-ins and a chance to go shopping in town and, most importantly, no school.

I don't remember feeling this way before I started secondary school, but then primary school had been much less demanding. There had been little to no homework and, in retrospect, the whole atmosphere had felt a little less strict.

Not that my primary school teachers had been particularly nice either. My first ever teacher had resembled a witch - she was a large woman, with (and

I'm not making this up, I swear) a prominent wart on her nose. Her physical appearance might not have mattered if she'd had a nice, child friendly personality - but she didn't and I was terrified of her from the first day, especially after she told another boy to go and stand in the corner after he'd been messing about in class.

My luck with teachers went downhill from there. My next teacher was the complete opposite of the previous one: young, blonde and pretty but seemingly just as unfriendly as the last - at least to me, who she seemed to take an almost immediate dislike to. I was constantly told off for being slow in my classwork, and for my terrible handwriting and was once sent to the headmistress for having drawn on the covers of my exercise books - that's exercise books, *not textbooks.*

Moving to secondary school, however, was to take my loathing of school and teachers up another notch. My secondary school was a faith-based one where, at least in the first two years, students were expected to attend a compulsory mass once a week. My mum wasn't religious, it was simply the best school nearby. In fact, I'd hardly been in a church since my christening and had to take my first communion at 10, in order to be allowed to attend.

Despite their supposed adherence to Christian beliefs, many of the teachers seemed far from it in their behaviour towards the pupils. Here, we were supposed to stand up whenever a teacher entered the room, be quiet unless we were spoken to and generally given the impression that we were less students, more inmates of some bizarre prison system where we were forced to learn.

Failure to comply with any of the many rules got you detention. Then, if that didn't work, a report card that had to be signed by each of your teachers and then your parents at the end of the week. Beyond that, it was suspension and then expulsion. Detentions were handed out by the teachers themselves and report cards generally by your form tutor, but suspensions and expulsions meant a visit to the Headmaster, Mr Felton.

A bluff, slightly portly man from the North, he'd manage to retain his accent despite many years of living "*down south*". Although he always seemed gruff and unfriendly to me, he did apparently have a more sensitive side. His "hands on approach" had led to several female sixth formers referring to him as '*One Up*' (as in '*felt one up*'). The name had stuck and was soon adopted by the majority of the student body (and, rumour had it, some of the teaching staff as well). Seeing as I obviously wasn't 'his type' and was generally the sort of student who tried to keep their head down, I rarely had any dealings with him.

Hence my surprise when my form tutor told me that I was to report to his office at once.

"Why does he want to see me, miss?"

"That's for him to know and you to find out, Robert. Now cut along there at once!"

I stood up, taking my bag with me, and made my way across to the main school building, where the headmaster's office was located on the first floor landing of the main staircase.

Many times in the past I'd seen some worried-looking student, sitting on the chairs outside the frosted glass door with Felton's name written on it as the whole school walked by and felt sympathy for them. Today, after first informing his secretary that I'd arrived, it was my turn to take a seat and await my fate.

I t was 1987. I had been at the school for about seven years. I'd decided to stay on and do my A-levels there because, basically, there didn't seem much point in going anywhere else. Most of my friends had done the same.

Joining Sixth-form had meant the arrival of a little bit more freedom, including the time during the day without lessons, in what were laughingly known as "study periods" - because that's what you were supposed to be doing during them - the teachers got very irate at anyone describing them as a "free period".

Regardless of when they were during the day, even if it was the first two hours in the morning like that Monday, you were still expected to turn up to registration and be in the school building for them. The reason given for this was to be able to know exactly how many sixth formers might be on the premises in the event of a fire, but in reality it was just another stupid rule to exert some control over students who were fast reaching an age where they could no longer be treated like children, in the same way that the teachers continued to expect us to address them by their surnames, rather than their christian names as the teachers in other sixth forms did.

The exception to the study period rule was Wednesday afternoons, where students were allowed to leave the school grounds provided they signed out on a register and gave some sort of reason. As the register was never checked, it soon became clear that students could give whatever reason they wanted, as long as the protocol was observed. Cue any number of amusing reasons why a student didn't need to be there. My personal favourites were *visiting the Great Wall Of China* and *rewiring the Kremlin*.

There were ways around the restrictions, however, even when it wasn't a Wednesday afternoon. A favourite trick for many, including myself, was to sign in to the school library, drop your bag by the door and head downstairs, claiming you were going to the computer room, when in fact you'd gone out through the fire exit door at the bottom of the stairs and come out by the main school gate. It was exactly what I'd been planning to do that morning. Once out of the gate, I'd head up the road to the local park, and pop into the cafe there for a bacon sandwich and a cup of tea. As acts of rebellion go, it was hardly earth-shattering, but it would have still gotten me in plenty of trouble if I'd been caught.

My thoughts about about the late breakfast I'd now never get to have were interrupted by the appearance of Mr Felton's head around the frosted glass door.

"Robert? Come in and sit down, lad…"

He ushered me into the office, whose large bay window offered the headmaster an enviable view of almost the entire playing field and woods beyond. A smartly dressed woman in her early 30s stood up as I came in.

"This is D.S. Morell, Robert."

The woman extended her hand to me. "Pleased to meet you, Robert. Erm…have we met before?"

I shook her hand, a little uncertainly. "No I don't think so. I don't think I've ever actually met a policeman…or policewoman for that matter. I'm sure that I'd remember if I had. Why?"

"Your face just looks familiar that's all, habit of the job, I guess." She smiled, as if to reassure me. It was a nice smile, but I still felt uneasy.

"I know the feeling, Detective Sergeant," said Felton. "I see faces all day long. Sometimes I get them mixed up too."

"Am I in some kind of trouble?" I asked.

"No, nothing like that," said Felton. "The Detective Sergeant just wants to ask you some questions that's all."

"Exactly," replied D.S. Morell. "Won't you take a seat, Robert?"

I sat down in the chair opposite the Detective Sergeant and Felton resumed his seat on the other side of the desk, across from us.

"Do you know a young woman called Claire Lambert, Robert?"

"Yes, is she ok?"

"She's been missing since Saturday," Morell replied. "Do you have any idea where she might have gone?"

"No, why should I?"

"It's my understanding that the two of you are quite close."

"Well, we're friends..."

"Just friends?"

I wasn't sure where to look. I felt Felton's eyes boring into me as much as Morell's.

"We liked each other..."

"Did you have a physical relationship?"

"What's that got to do with anything?"

"Just answer the bloody question, Robert!" Felton thundered.

"Yes! ok? We had a physical relationship...does he really need to be here for this?" I asked Morell, indicating Felton.

"May I remind you, you're sitting in my office, young man..." Felton began, but Morell cut him short.

"Perhaps it might be better if I could talk to Robert alone, for a few minutes, Headmaster?"

"I really don't think that's..."

"I realise it's an imposition, but it might be for the best. Just for a few minutes? Perhaps you could ask your secretary to make us a cup of coffee and maybe Robert might like a glass of water?"

"I would, actually."

"Well, in that case, I'll just see to that. How do you take your coffee Detective Sergeant?"

"Milk, no sugar - thank you, Headmaster." She smiled at him as he got up from his desk and went out the door.

"Thank goodness, I thought he'd never leave..." I must have looked surprised. "Relax, Rob. It is 'Rob' isn't it? Or do you prefer 'Robbie'? I'm sure most people don't call you 'Robert'."

"Only the teachers here and my Mum when she's angry."

This garnered a smile from Morell. "Does she need to get angry with you often?"

I shrugged. "No more than any other Mum with a seventeen year old son does, I guess."

"Well, you're not in any trouble, ok? Now, tell me about Claire. The two of you were going out together?"

"We'd not been seeing each other that long. Do you think she's been abducted?"

Morell held up her hand. "She's just missing. No-one's seen her since Saturday. That's all I know. Her Mum said you were at the house on Friday, is that correct?"

I nodded.

"Was everything ok between you and Claire?"

"Yes..." I hesitated slightly, not sure if should I say more.

Morell noticed. "The two of you had sex?"

"Yes."

"And afterwards?"

"We talked for a bit."

"About?"

"This and that. Music mostly."

"Ah yes, she writes songs - her Mum told me. You're also in a band, I gather. Is that how the two of you met?"

"No, I knew her when she used to go to school here, but we didn't really become friends until after she left and I saw her playing one night at the *Jack And Jill*."

"The pub opposite the station?"

"They have an open mic night, first Thursday of the month. Glen and I were playing there as well."

"Glen Matthews? He goes to school here too, right?"

"Yes. He's my best friend."

"Is he friends with Claire as well?"

"Sort of, he's talked to her a few times...but it's not like the three of us hang out together."

"I understand. So, you and Claire talked for a while, then what?"

"I said "*goodbye*" and left."

"What time was this?"

"About 5.30. I needed to get home in time for dinner."

"Did she say anything to you about what she was planning to do over the weekend?"

"No, she said she might call me on Sunday afternoon."

"Did she?"

"No."

"And this didn't bother you?"

"Well, a bit..."

"But you didn't think to call her?"

"No, I figured she'd just forgotten. She didn't say for definite that she'd call. Anyway, I just assumed she was busy doing homework, like I was and I'd hear from her today or tomorrow. Glen and I are playing at *Pow!* on Wednesday night and she said she'd come along to the gig. I wasn't worried."

"Playing it cool, huh? The old *'treat 'em mean, keep 'em keen'* routine?"

"I'm not like that."

"No?"

"No."

"So, the two of you had sex and then talked for a while - according to you, about nothing much and certainly nothing about the possibility that she might go somewhere over the weekend - when she doesn't call you on Sunday, you're not worried and don't try and call her. You can see my problem surely, Rob? It's hard for me to believe that something didn't happen between you on Friday that led to her going missing. Did the two of you have a fight?"

"No, I told you - everything was fine. I saw it was getting late and I said "*goodbye*" and left. That was all, I swear."

Morell still didn't look like she believed me. She looked like she was about to press me some more on my relationship with Claire, but at that moment Mr Felton returned with the coffee and the glass of water.

"Thank you very much, Mr Felton," she said as she sipped the coffee and I gulped back a bit of the cold water, "we're actually almost done here. Tell me a bit about yourself, Rob, what are you studying for A-Level?"

"English, History and I.T."

"That's computers," the headmaster explained. Morell ignored him.

"Do you play computer games a lot?"

"Not that much, I'm more interested in programming, to be honest. Computers are beginning to be used in music too, so it's that sort of thing that I'm most interested in."

"That sounds quite cutting edge."

"We have a brand new computer room, in the basement, if you'd like a tour on your way out Detective Sergeant?" Felton cut in. "It's all a little beyond me, I'm afraid, I'm still struggling with the electric typewriter...".

"I know quite a bit about computers," Morell replied. "My father's a computer programmer, in fact."

Felton looked decidedly crestfallen.

"Would you be able to create music programs as part of the course, then?"

"That's probably a bit advanced for me at the moment. Right now, we're trying to program our own simple adaptations of Conway's *Game Of Life*."

"The students also learn skills other than just programming games, of course..." the headmaster began, but Morell interrupted him again.

"Conway's *'Life'* isn't really a game, in the traditional sense, headmaster. In fact, it doesn't need any players - it runs itself. Conway was the mathematician who invented it. It's not even really to do with computers at all, it's about cellular automata, but it does have some important applications to programming. Basically, you have a grid full of cells, which can only have two possible states: alive or dead.

There are a bunch of rules: any cell with two or three live cells as neighbours stays alive, any dead cell with three live neighbours comes back to life and any live cells that don't fit this criteria die off and obviously the ones that already dead stay that way unless they now have live cells next to them,"

"It sounds rather brutal…" Felton replied, clearly only able to understand a fragment of what Morell had just explained to him.

"It's really about how a very small set of rules or conditions can create seemingly complex systems." I chimed in. "Those few rules mean a constantly changing grid, that runs until it has played out every possible permutation of cells. If the grid was infinite, then the game would never end."

"So how big a grid are you currently working with?" Morell asked.

"Only one of 20 x 20 cells, but that's still enough to have the program run quite a while before it exhausts all the possible permutations."

"Very interesting. Anyway, I'll let you get back to class, but perhaps I could ask you to contact me on this number, if you think of anything more." She handed me a card. "Anything…anything at all. Equally, if you hear from Claire or you notice anything out of the ordinary, let me know, ok? Her mum's worried about her."

"Of course."

"Very well, that's all then," she replied, nodding to Felton.

"Thank you, Robert, you may go back to class," Felton said to me.

I didn't wait to be told twice. I finished my plastic beaker of water, picked up my bag and left.

I found Glen waiting for me in the cafeteria.

"Hello stranger," he said as I plonked my bag down on the table and slumped into the plastic chair next to him. "What did '*One Up*' want?" Glen was in the same form as me and we'd been sitting next to each when I'd been summoned to the headmaster's office earlier. Naturally, he was curious to know what it had all been about.

"It wasn't Felton who wanted to see me," I replied, trying to keep my voice relatively low, "it was the police."

"What?"

"There was this policewoman waiting for me in Felton's office, D.S. Morell, she said her name was. Look…" I fished the card Morell had given me out of my pocket and showed it to him.

"Fuck! What did she want?"

"Claire is missing."

"Seriously?"

"Yes, no-one's seen her since Saturday, apparently."

"Shit! Her poor Mum must be going out of her mind."

"I know. I just don't understand it, this isn't like her at all."

"And she said nothing to you about it?"

"Of course not!"

"But you saw her on Friday…"

"Yes and when I left her everything was fine. She said she'd call me on Sunday, but she didn't."

"And you didn't call her?"

"No. I meant to but then I had to get that history essay finished for today and then by the time I was done it was getting late."

"That sounds pretty lame."

"Thanks. The police just told me the same thing."

"Well it does. I mean, you were fucking her - I'm guessing that's what the two of you were doing on Friday afternoon, right? Fucking?"

"Don't say it like that."

"Like what?"

"You make it sound like something I should be ashamed of."

"Are you?"

"Am I what?"

"Ashamed?"

"No. Why, are you jealous?

"Of you?"

"Of her."

"What's this? A lover's tiff?" Our voices had gotten louder and we hadn't noticed Ollie Harding and his pal, Mario, walk over to where we were sitting. "Hey, Rob, what did '*One Up*' want with you? Is he going to expel you for being a poof?"

"Piss off, Ollie, I'm not in the mood..."

"Don't you fucking tell me to 'piss off' you little gay boy!"

"Oh yeah? What are you gonna do about it? You're already on report this week - you start anything with me, you'll be suspended." After the questioning I'd had from D.S. Morell, little shits like Ollie Harding didn't scare me as much as they would normally do.

"Maybe I don't care about being suspended," Ollie replied, leaning closer to me. He'd clearly just been off somewhere smoking a cigarette - even though it was forbidden on school grounds - I could smell it on his breath.

"How about arrested then? Felton hauled me into his office to talk to the police - they're probably still on the grounds - you hit me, it won't just be a school matter, it'll be a police one."

"Bollocks! What would the coppers want with you?"

"There's been a lot of reports of homophobic abuse and bullying at the school, Felton's taking it seriously and has called in the police."

"No he fucking hasn't!"

"It's true," Glen chimed in. "Rob's just told me - here's the card the police gave him if you don't believe him." He held out the card for Ollie to read.

"That's no good, Glen, you'll have to read it to him - it'll take too long otherwise…"

"Oi! You calling me 'thick'?" Ollie said, leaning towards me again.

"No, I'm calling you 'illiterate', fuckwit - there's a difference."

"Don't you call me a 'fuckwit', you little ponce or I'll break your face!" Ollie replied, raising his fist towards me.

"If you touch me it means you love me…"

This stopped Ollie short. "You're a fucking queer, just like your bum boy friend here. You've probably both got AIDS. I wouldn't touch you with a ten foot pole."

"Aww, bet you say that to all the boys, Ollie." I blew him a kiss. He raised his fist again but Mario held him back and the two of them walked away.

"Fucking *hell*, what's got into you today?" Glen said once they'd gone. I thought I could hear a note of admiration in his voice.

"C'mon," I replied, "let's get out of here."

It was obviously too late to head up to the cafe now, so instead we made our way out on to the playing fields. It was a sunny day so there were quite a few sixth formers sitting around on the grass or on the wooden benches and tables that were dotted around, but we didn't sit down there and instead made our way towards the small wooded area that stood in front of most of the lower wall of the school grounds. Strictly speaking, we weren't allowed to be here. No student was supposed to enter the woods unless instructed to by a teacher and then only during sports lessons. The P.E. teachers seemed to take some kind of sadistic pleasure in having younger students run, in freezing cold weather, round the entire perimeter of the school in shorts and a t-shirt. Fortunately, those days were over now that we were in the sixth form and Glen and I often snuck in there. There were two sets of benches and tables not far from the entrance to the woods, so we made a beeline towards them and then at the last minute, swerved off into the trees.

There was a small grotto at the edge of the woods, which I'd always found slightly creepy and which was certainly an odd thing to have in the grounds of a school, but that's how it was. We walked past it and sat down on the branches of a low tree on the raised mound that formed the top of the grotto. Glen took out a pack of cigarettes and offered me one, but I shook my head and instead took out a joint that I had stuffed down my sock that morning and lit it.

"Wow, that bad huh?" he said after I'd taken two long tokes on the joint and passed it to him.

"It sucks." I exhaled slowly, feeling the weed take hold.

"You were something else with Ollie. I've never seen you like that."

"Yeah, well, bigger fish to fry…"

"Meaning?"

"Meaning, I'm even less tolerant of that little wanker's bullshit than usual."

"You still need to be careful, he won't forget that and you may have just painted a great big target on your back."

"As if I care. I mean, he's not going to actually do anything is he?"

No? What happens if you and I bump into him and his mates outside of school? You know how small this town is, it's bound to happen eventually."

"I can look after myself, so can you."

"He's just the sort of little psycho to walk around with a knife in his pocket."

"I don't think even he'd be that stupid."

"I wouldn't put anything past him."

There was nothing to say to this. Despite the bravado I'd shown in the cafeteria, Glen wasn't kidding. Ollie Harding wasn't just a school bully, you had a sense that he could be really dangerous. If you met him outside of school, particularly if he had a bunch of mates with him that he felt he needed to look 'hard' in front of, then you might be in real trouble. At that moment, however, part of me would have only too happily tried to beat the shit out of him, even if though I would have come out the loser.

Claire.

She was the reason I was feeling this way, right now. This wasn't like her at all.

I thought back to Friday afternoon.

We'd met in the park, smoked a joint and gone back to her house. It was only the second time I'd ever been there. She lived in one of those three storey Regency houses, where you go up a set of steps to the front door. Most of these had long since been split into flats, but astonishingly Claire's parents had bought the entire house. She told me that her Mum and Dad had separated two years earlier and he now lived somewhere else. Claire had somehow managed to convince her Mum to let her have the entire basement floor - which was huge, like our front room and kitchen combined - for herself.

She'd redecorated it and the walls were now covered with posters, including a huge one of Bowie looking ultra cool, lying in bed smoking a cigarette, one arm tucked behind his head, which hung on the wall beside her bed. The bed, which was a futon that she folded up and used like a sofa otherwise, was next to the big bay window, which looked out on to the steps that lead down to the tiny basement courtyard and door (yes, she even had her own front door - though she generally use the main front door upstairs). A small bedside table with a whole pile of books piled next to it, was next to the futon. Opposite this was her stereo and a shelving unit with hundreds of tapes and still more books on it, with a chair and a small desk next to it, where she did her homework. The bay window had a window seat, which she'd piled high with cushions and was her favourite place to sit.

At the far end of the room, in front of the window that looked out onto the back garden, she'd set up a little home studio for herself, tacking up some old duvets up against part of the the wall to create a homemade vocal booth. She had two SM58 microphones, one to record her singing and another, set at about waist height, to record her acoustic guitar. The cables from the microphones trailed very neatly across the floor (she'd even taped them down in a few places) to a small desk, where she had a little Yamaha keyboard, an old Sequential drum machine and most impressively of all: a Tascam Portastudio 4-track.

The first time I'd gone there and seen her amazing room, I'd been speechless. My bedroom was tiny in comparison and clearly the level of belief that her Mum showed in Claire and her music was staggering. My own Mum - who continually complained about my messy bedroom, with my guitar invariably perched precariously against the bed, records and tapes and books overflowing from virtually every shelf and a desk which I could never work at, because it was constantly covered with stuff - would never have shown me this sort of support. Only recently, when I'd talked about doing some sort of music technology or sound engineering course, once I finished my A-levels, she'd told me *"music is just a phase you'll grow out of"*. Even Glen's mum, who was much more accommodating than mine when it came to her son's passion for music, wouldn't have given him over part of the house so that he and I could play and record our music. In fact, most of the time we'd generally end up rehearsing in his living room.

Claire and I had said "*hello*" to her Mum, briefly, before going downstairs to Claire's room in the basement. We'd taken off our shoes and Claire had put a Pet Shop Boys tape on. Then she'd sat down next to me on the futon and we'd started kissing. I'd put my hand underneath her top and felt her breasts and then we'd broken apart for a moment whilst she removed first her top and then mine.

"Hang on," she said, and got up and went over to the door and locked it.

"Your mum doesn't mind you doing that?" I asked, knowing that my Mum would have a fit if I'd brought a girl home, taken her up to my room and locked the door.

"Locking the door? Why should she?" she replied, as if it was the most natural thing in the world. "Anyway, it's more to stop Tom barging in here, asking if he can borrow a tape or something."

Tom was Claire's younger brother, whom I'd yet to meet. He was thirteen and although Claire clearly thought a great deal of him, he could apparently also be a bit of a nuisance when she had friends over.

She came back to the futon and took off her bra and her jeans and slid underneath the duvet. "Come on," she said, "it's nice and warm under here."

I took off my jeans and socks and got under the duvet with her. We kissed some more and I could feel myself getting hard, as I felt her breasts pressing against my chest. She could feel it too and pushed her hips closer to mine.

"I think we've still got too many clothes on..." she said, pulling away from me slightly.

She slipped off her underwear and I stood up again and pulled off my boxer shorts, whilst she opened a drawer in the bedside table and pulled out a condom. "Shall I put it on for you?"

I nodded. I'd never actually put one on before, except in a sex education lesson at school and then we'd had to place it over a banana - which wasn't really the same thing. We'd never gotten this far together. The previous time we'd been alone in her room, there'd been a lot of kissing and rubbing and then at the end she'd taken me in her mouth. I hoped my erection would hold as she gently rolled the condom on to my cock. Then I lay back on the bed whilst she eased herself on top of me. After all the foreplay we both came fairly quickly. When we were done, she bent forward and kissed me one more time before rolling off and lying next to me, sweaty and breathless.

"That was your first time, wasn't it?" she asked, once she'd got her breath back.

"Was it that obvious?"

"No, it was fine...I just guessed that's all."

"I'm guessing it wasn't yours?"

She shook her head. "Does it matter?"

"Of course not."

"It feels special to be your first. You'll never forget me."

"As if I would anyway!"

I pulled off the condom, wrapped it in a tissue along with the wrapper and put it in the pocket of my jeans.

"What are you doing?"

"Well, I didn't want your Mum to find it..."

"Don't be silly, Rob - just put it in the bin and come back here."

I did as I was told and got back underneath the duvet cover with her. She laid her head against my chest and I stroked the short hair at the nape of her neck. She cut it shorter now than she had when we'd been at school together. It suited her and made her look a little like Gillian Gilbert or Tracy Thorn.

To be honest, I think I'd fallen for her that first time I'd seen her again at the *Jack and Jill*. I could barely believe it was the same girl who'd sat across from me in French and History a year or so before. I'm ashamed to say I hadn't really noticed her back then and it wasn't as if we'd had a lot of friends in common. Which made it all the more surprising when she seemed genuinely pleased to see me at the bar afterwards.

"Rob? Is that you?"

"Yeah, Hi! How are you? You were amazing up there, I had no idea you were a singer - how long have you been writing your own songs?"

"A while, but it's only recently I've really plucked up the courage to try and go out and perform them."

"They were brilliant, have you got many more?"

"Notebooks full of them, but a lot of them are crap. I'm always writing new stuff, though."

"You going to Faber sixth-form now, right?"

"Yeah, what about you?"

"Still at St. John's - though I probably should've done the same as you did."

Out of the corner of my eye I saw Glen, gesturing that we needed to get ready as we were on next. "Listen, are you sticking around for a bit? I've got to go and play but it would be great to have a drink and catch up afterwards."

"Sure."

"Ok, great - see you after."

I went up to the stage with Glen, picked up my guitar and after checking that it was still in tune and making sure my synth was set to the right sound, I looked over to Glen to see if he was ready. He nodded, I started the drum machine and we were off into our first song.

Claire was as good as her word, not only did she stick around, she joined the group near the front of the stage listening intently to the music. When the first song ended, she cheered the loudest and I found myself directing my entire performance towards her that evening. Every time I looked up from either my guitar or synth I wondered if she might be looking somewhere else, but every time I did I found her looking straight back into my eyes. This unbroken connection continued throughout the entire set and I felt as if I was playing just for her.

Afterwards, Glen and I went over to the bar and chatted to Claire for a while. She was really complimentary about our short set, the songs and especially Glen's voice. The topic then changed to St. John's and we filled her in about the latest gossip on the various teachers and pupils that she known when she was there. Eventually, Glen made his excuses and left, but Claire and I stayed on until closing time and ended up sharing a cab together, as I had both my guitar and the synth to take home with me and we discovered that we didn't live that far from each other.

"I always knew you'd go somewhere with your music," she said to me, as we were waiting for the taxi. "I remember hearing you and Glen practicing at lunchtime up the music department when we were in the 4th year and you were already really good, even then."

"Why didn't you say something?"

"I dunno," she shrugged, "it was never the right moment, I guess."

She leaned in and kissed me and I was only too happy to reciprocate because I'd been wanting to kiss her most of the evening. The way she looked, her voice, the things she sang about. Later, I found myself thinking back about every little detail. When the taxi arrived and we got in and gave the driver her address. I found myself reaching for her hand in the darkness of the backseat and she held on to my fingers lightly, before breaking contact, reaching into her guitar bag, pulling out a biro and writing her phone number on my hand. When we reached her house she leant forward to the driver and gave him her share of the fare.

"Give me a call, tomorrow," she said, as she got out with her guitar.

And I did.

"Do you want to talk about it?" Glen asked me and I realised that I'd been quiet for some time. There were tears in my eyes. I dried them and shook my head.

"There's nothing to tell. I'm just scared something's happened to her, that's all."

I don't know what made me look up at that moment but, as I did, I spotted a boy of about 11 or 12, a little further off in the woods. He was wearing the maroon jumper and grey trousers that the 1st and 2nd years wore and he was looking straight at Glen and I.

"What are you doing? You're not supposed to be here!"

"Who are you shouting at?" Glen asked, looking in the boy's direction.

"Some 1st year watching us..." I got up and walked towards the boy, but as I got a closer, he turned and walked away. I tried to catch up with him but the path through the woods twists and turns quite a bit and soon I'd lost sight of him. I broke into a run, but it was no use - the boy had gone. I suddenly began to feel as if I'd lost my bearings, slightly. I didn't remember the woods being this dense or having so many different paths in it and I was quite relieved when Glen finally caught up with me.

"What the hell are you doing? Why did you go running off like that?"

"I was trying to catch up with that 1st year."

"What are you talking about?"

"The one that was watching us."

"All I saw was you shouting and then you got up and ran off."

"You mean you didn't see him?"

"No. What's the matter with you, today?"

"I dunno."

But that was a lie. I knew exactly what was bothering me: *I'd seen that same boy before and now I remembered where.*

There are lots of people who find seaside towns really cool. Certainly, if you only visit them on a sunny Bank Holiday weekend, then it's easy to be lured into thinking how wonderful it must be to live in such a place all year 'round. It's only when you've spent a wet and windy week in one, when the sky, the sea and the concrete buildings blur into one another, that you realise that seaside towns can also be some of the most depressing places on earth.

The heavens opened around lunchtime, but despite that I went down to the town centre once school finished at 3:15.

I asked Glen if he wanted to come along, but he told me he needed to go home and practice the piece that he had to perform in his music lesson the following day. I understood this completely. Mr Tiller, the head of the music department didn't like Glen. He didn't like me either, for that matter, but, as I'd stopped studying music after O-level, I wasn't his problem anymore. He once told me in a rare moment of candour that two things he really disliked were *"improvisation and electric guitars."* As I was fond of both, it was clear we were never going to get along. Glen was different though, he'd actually taken piano lessons and understood music theory - or at least a lot more than I did - and he'd elected to study Music for A-level, yet for some reason Tiller and he didn't see eye to eye, either. Whether it was Glen's taste in music, which was quite eclectic, or the fact that he made no attempt to disguise what I heard one teacher describe in snide terms as his *"flamboyant nature"*, Tiller would often claim that Glen's work just wasn't good enough.

Most students would have given up, but Glen had a stubborn streak in him and instead of trying to appease Tiller, he simply found more and more elaborate ways to annoy him - choosing to write pieces in unusual scales, sometimes featuring rapid key changes and even, on one occasion, non-standard notation. Despite or rather because of this, he was extra careful to make sure that his performances of these daring new compositions would be flawless. He knew Tiller would be eagerly following the score on paper as Glen played it and would surely use any deviation from it as an excuse to bring Glen's marks down, even further. So he went home to practice some more and I caught the number seven bus into town.

I went into Virgin Megastore on the high street. I looked at the new albums and the videos on the ground floor, before heading up the escalator to the first floor with the in-store radio station, cassettes and the t-shirts. I browsed around there for a bit, then went up the next flight of steps, past the mezzanine cafe, up to the top floor where they had the rest of the records, as well as the books and posters. I checked out a couple of the new releases on the headphone listening stations there and toyed with buying a *Blade Runner* poster. I also glanced through the latest issues of the *NME*, *Melody Maker* and even *Smash Hits*, which I still liked because they printed the lyrics to many of the songs in the top 40.

After that, I made my way along to the main shopping centre in Winston Square. Built in the early

70s, it was a brutalist concrete quadrangle, with shops on all sides, leading down ramps or escalators to car parks for those carrying back their weekly shopping from Sainsbury's or Waitrose. There was also an HMV, an Our Price and a W.H. Smith's, which is where I was headed. Next door to the W.H. Smith's was the clothes shop that Claire worked in on Saturdays. I knew this because I'd stopped off to meet her there a couple of times on my home from my own Saturday job at the local library.

The last time I'd visited her at the shop, I'd almost bumped into a boy of about eleven coming out, just as I was walking in. At first I'd wondered if it might have been Claire's brother Tom but when I mentioned it to her, she shook her head.

"He's just a boy I know - I help him with his Maths homework sometimes."

"He comes to visit you at work?"

"Sometimes - he's clearly got a bit of a crush on me. It's rather sweet really."

"Sounds a bit creepy to me."

"He's eleven, Rob."

"And? I'm sure my thoughts about girls weren't all that pure at eleven!"

"I'll bet they weren't!" she said with a smirk. "I'll be another ten minutes at least, do you want to wait for me outside?"

"Sure."

I left her to finish closing up the shop and by the time she eventually came out, I'd pretty much forgotten about the boy altogether.

Until I'd seen him again in the woods, that morning.

I stopped outside the shop and looked in the window. I was briefly considering going inside to ask about Claire, but thought better of it and as I turned away I almost collided with D.S. Morell.

"Hello Rob, fancy seeing you, here. This is where Claire works isn't it?"

"Er...yes, on Saturdays."

"Today's Monday."

"I know. I was just walking past the shop and I was thinking about going in and asking about Claire."

"You'd be wasting your time. They have no idea where she is either - she didn't turn up for work on Saturday."

"So she disappeared on her way to work?"

"We don't know. When her Mum didn't see her on Saturday morning, she just assumed that Claire had already left for work and didn't start to worry until she didn't come home that evening. Do you have a Saturday job?"

"Yes, I work in the library."

"Were you working there this Saturday?"

"Yes, of course."

"That's not far from here, did you come up and visit Claire when she was working? In your lunch hour or after work, maybe?"

"Sometimes."

"But not this last Saturday?"

"You just said she wasn't working here on Saturday..."

"But you didn't know that."

"Of course not."

"So, why didn't you come and visit her?"

"I just didn't. It's not like I came to visit her every week."

Morell studied me for a few moments. "Ok," she said.

"Does that mean I can go?"

"Of course."

She moved aside and I walked off quickly towards HMV. I hadn't really planned to go in there having seen pretty much all I wanted to see in the Virgin Megastore, but I didn't want to hang around and answer any more of Morell's questions either, so I went off in the opposite direction than the one I'd been planning to.

As soon as I turned the corner I knew I'd made a mistake.

Sitting around the fountain in the middle of the square's quadrangle were Ollie, Mario and another couple of lads who went to our school but whose names I couldn't remember.

They saw me instantly and with a shout that echoed around the buildings in the square, they got up and ran towards me.

I didn't even stop to think. I just turned and ran.

I shot down the escalators and turned left into the car park. I could hear them closing in behind me, and dropped down behind a Ford Escort. I knew I needed to get to the back of the car park, where there was a staircase leading up to the walkway across to the other car park beyond. If I could get there I'd be able to lose them easily, as there were a bunch of different exits I could take. I heard them run, panting, into the car park and stop to catch their breath.

"Where the fuck did he go?" I heard one of them ask.

"He's hiding in here, just spread out and look for him" Ollie replied.

"Aww just leave it Ollie, there's no point now." That was Mario. "He's pretty fucking fast, I'll give him that."

"Yeah," said one of the others who was still gasping for breath. "He should be in the bloody Olympics, that one."

"Just shut up all of you!" Ollie snapped. "There's no way he made it out the back, he's just probably hiding behind one of the cars. Spread out, we'll find him."

"And then what?" You can't kick the shit out of him here, there's too many people around."

"We'll see about that!"

"Si's right, Ollie," said Mario. "There's too many people around, we should leave it."

"I know you can hear me, you little prick!" Ollie shouted to the garage. "I'm going to catch up with you sooner or later and when I do, you're fucking dead!"

His words bounced off the concrete walls of the car park with a high pitched slap. He waited until it was quiet again and then he and the others turned around and went back the way they came. I sat there quietly behind the Escort for a few more minutes to make absolutely sure they'd gone before getting up and making my way over to the staircase. Once I'd crossed into the next car park, I strolled out the bottom exit that led down to the sea front. I walked along the promenade until I reached Palmerston Square and cut through there, back up to the high street, where I managed to catch a number seven bus that was just coming past. It was only once I'd taken my seat on the top deck that I realised I was shaking.

Once I got home, I tried my best to concentrate on my English essay on unreliable narrators, but it was no use. I couldn't even enjoy *The Lenny Henry Show*, which normally would have had me in hysterics, because the actress in it reminded me a little bit of Claire and that got me thinking about her again. So I switched it off halfway through and said to my Mum that I was going for a walk around the block.

I told myself afterwards that I hadn't really intended to walk past Claire's house that evening, that I was just wandering aimlessly around the neighbourhood and ended up there more or less by accident - but who am I kidding? Consciously or otherwise I knew I needed to go past the house, maybe even talk to her Mum, though I certainly didn't relish the prospect.

When I got there, however, the whole house was dark. I stood watching it for a few moments from across the street and then crossed over the road, went up the steps to the front door and rang the doorbell. I could hear it echoing inside the house but there was no sound of movement from within and no lights came on. Nobody was home. I walked back and turned down the steps that led down to Claire's part of the house in the basement. I peered in at the window but it was too dark to really see anything inside. As I turned around to go back up the steps, someone shone a flashlight in my face.

I nearly jumped out of my skin.

"Is that you, Rob?" D.S. Morell's voice said from behind the flashlight. "We really must stop meeting like this, you know?"

"Funnily enough, I was just about to say the same thing." I replied, shielding my eyes from the glare of the flashlight. "Are you following me Detective Sergeant?

"Not at all, we just seem to turn up at the same places all the time. Do you mind telling me what you're doing here?"

It had been stupid to come to the house. I should have known that Morell might be waiting for me, but I wasn't about to tell her that. "I'm looking for Claire, that should be pretty self-explanatory shouldn't it?"

"She's missing. Why would you come and look for her, here?"

"I don't know. I thought I'd come and talk to her Mum, maybe"

"Her Mum isn't home."

"I can see that."

"But you thought come and check out the house anyway? I hope you weren't thinking about breaking in?"

"Of course not."

"So what were you doing?"

"Where are Claire's mum and her younger brother?"

"Why?"

"Just curious. It seems a little odd that with her daughter missing, Mrs Lambert would be anywhere else other than waiting by the phone, doesn't it?"

"You're right. It's almost as odd as Claire's boyfriend turning up at her house and peering through the windows when it's clear there's no one home. Come up from down there, please..."

I made my way back up the steps, still with the flashlight in my eyes, and half stumbled through the wrought iron gate.

"You're barking up the wrong tree, if you think I had anything to do with Claire going missing. When I left her here on Friday afternoon, she was fine. She didn't say anything about going anywhere, we didn't have a fight, she wasn't depressed or anything - she was fine."

"And yet she is *missing*. You know what I think, Rob? I think the reason why you weren't worried about her not calling you on Sunday, is the exactly the same reason why you didn't go and visit her at work on Saturday - some part of you knew she wouldn't be there if you tried to call or went to visit her. That's the only plausible explanation for your sudden lack of interest in her."

"It's not that at all..." I started to say, but then stopped. No matter what I said it was pretty clear Morell wouldn't believe me. "Do you know where Claire's mum has gone or when she might be back? I'd like to speak to her."

"No, I don't. What do you want to ask her?"

"I just want to talk to her about Claire."

"Her mum doesn't know where she's gone, Rob, I've already told you that and I don't think you'll be very welcome if you turn up and start asking questions. Do yourself a favour and stay away from Claire's family and this house, ok?"

"Ok."

"You told me that you and Glen are playing a gig on Wednesday evening. Where did you say it was?"

"At Pow! - it's in the arches, down by the seafront. We're supporting The Rayguns."

"What time does it start?"

"Why are you going to come along?"

"That's right. Don't look so surprised, Rob, I'm not that old..."

"Er..no, it's not that..."

"So, what time?"

"Well, we're on first - obviously, as we're the support act. I think the doors open at 7.30 and we go on at 8."

"What's your band called?"

"*Teenage Wildlife.*"

"After the Bowie track on *Scary Monsters*?"

"Yes, you like Bowie?"

"I practically grew up on Bowie, my Dad's a massive fan of his. Fine, I'll see you there. Now get off home."

I did as I was told and left D.S. Morell standing there outside Claire's house. I didn't go straight home, however. I took the long way 'round, underneath the railway viaduct. It was a route I took quite often, especially if wasn't in a hurry to get home.

At one side of the viaduct, there was a small gate with barbed wire over the top, that led to a set of steps going up to the railway line, about two hundred yards from the station. At this point, I told myself, the trains would still be travelling fairly slowly and many times I'd fantasised about climbing the gate, waiting up there next to the line and hopping aboard a train as it trundled slowly out of the station, not caring where it would take me. It was a stupid fantasy, of course, I'd be much more likely to get hit by a train, step on the third rail or end up being arrested for trespassing. If I wanted to get away, there were much simpler ways - I could just walk into the station and buy a ticket, but somehow I couldn't stop thinking about that gate and the steps behind it.

I crossed over to the gate and looked at it up close. It wasn't that big and there was a wall next to it with an overgrown grassy slope going up, that I could probably use to hoist myself up.

Not tonight though, I told myself and headed up the hill towards home.

II. UNDER PRESSURE

Glen merely raised his eyebrow and gave me the "*I told you so*" look, when I told him about the run in with Ollie and his mates in town, when we sitting in the cafe in the park at lunchtime the following day. He was much more alarmed about my two meetings with D.S. Morell and that she'd said she was going to come to our gig.

"That's a bit weird, don't you think? I mean, that doesn't feel like standard police procedure."

"You have no more idea about 'standard police procedure', than I do, Glen. There's no law against her turning up at a public event, is there?"

"It sounds as if she thinks you're a suspect."

"I am a suspect - I'm the boyfriend."

"She's just missing. It's not as if her body's not turned up, half-naked, strangled with her own bra..."

I laughed and almost choked on my bacon sandwich at Glen's lurid fantasy that could have come straight out of the tabloids, but it disturbed me as well. Claire going missing was bad enough, without the thought that something terrible might have happened to her.

We went back into the school via the fire exit opposite the computer lab. Just as I started to climb the steps up to the library, I heard Ollie's unmistakable voice at the top of the stairs.

"I'm telling you - that's *his* bag. He's probably downstairs in the computer lab, writing his stupid programs."

"What if he is? There's probably a teacher down there, so you can't start anything with him."

"We'll see."

I heard them start to walk down, so I turned around and almost collided with Glen.

"What the..." I put my hand up to his mouth and pulled him back out the fire exit just before Ollie and Mario came into view. A few seconds later and we'd have walked right into them. As soon as I was sure they'd gone into the computer lab and were no longer looking in our direction, Glen and I legged it up the stairs to the library, grabbed our bags and headed off in the direction of our lessons that afternoon. Neither of us said anything on the way, we didn't need to. Both of us knew what the other was thinking.

That had been too close for comfort.

G len had his performance in front of Mr Tiller in the last period that afternoon which meant he finished slightly later than I did. I'd agreed to go along and wait for him outside the music department, once my History lesson was over and then we'd catch the bus into town together as, in addition to working there on a Saturday, I also worked at the library from 5.30 until 7.30 on Tuesdays, when they stayed open later than usual. Sometimes, Glen came and hung out with me in the library whilst I was working.

After I'd stuck my head around the door of some of the practice rooms to see if any of the other music students we knew were about, I went over to the notice board to see if our poster for the gig had been torn down yet (it had - *surprise, surprise!*). I took a new poster from my bag and was just putting it up, when a photo from one of the school concerts caught my eye. There were several first year students holding instruments and the last one on the right of the picture I recognised immediately.

It was the boy who'd been in the woods the day before.

"You're not really supposed to put up posters for student bands up on the notice board, Robert."

I turned around to find Ms Timmons, who'd joined the music department when Glen and I had been doing our O-Levels, looking at me with raised eyebrows.

"I'm sorry miss," I replied, "was that why it had been taken down?"

"Probably. Though I will say it wasn't taken down by me."

"The gig's tomorrow, miss, it only has to stay up until then…it might mean a few more people come and see us."

"Alright," she sighed, "but don't blame me if Mr Tiller gets cross with you about it."

"Of course, thanks miss. By the way, you don't know who this boy is in this photo do you, by any chance?"

"Yes, that's my first year group and they're all girls."

I turned back to the photo I'd just been looking at and saw that she was right. There was no boy in the photo at all.

"Maybe, you've been having too many late nights with all those gigs you've been playing?"

I laughed nervously at her joke and was trying to think of something else to say, when Glen appeared.

"Right, the inquisition's over, we can go…"

"Glen, it's really not appropriate to compare your viva with the head of the music department as 'the inquisition', especially in a Christian school."

"Yes, sorry miss," Glen replied with all the mock contriteness he could muster. "I meant it affectionately."

"Yes, I'm sure you did, just as I'm sure you'll understand when I tell you that if I hear you use that phrase to describe your assessments with Mr Tiller again, you'll be in detention - is that clear?"

"Yes, miss…sorry."

"Off you go, then…"

On the bus into town, Glen told me that Tiller had been surprisingly complimentary about his piece, saying "he'd noticed some improvement" in Glen's playing.

He'd still only given him a 'C', though.

We got off at Winston Square and walked down through the town to where the library was. Glen had to return some books, so I left him at the entrance, whilst I went downstairs to the staff room to collect my assistant's badge and drop my school bag off.

My job consisted of the typical library assistant's duties (you can only be called "a librarian" if you've got a degree qualification): sitting behind the desk marking returned books back in and marking out those being borrowed, as well as shelving those that had been returned.

Thanks to my interest in music, I often ended up working in the music library, which was upstairs next to the reference section, when the official music librarian wasn't there and that's where I was working that afternoon. Working in the music library was exactly the same as working in the main library, except that the customers were generally a bit more snobbish and the inquiries (generally about whether we had a particular piece of sheet music or whether we had a specific recording of a classical composer's work) could be slightly more tricky. Which is why a knowledge of music was helpful - customers were known to become slightly irritated at having to spell Rimsky-Korsakov or Khachaturian, when making a request.

Personally, I always enjoyed worked there when I had the chance. There was less shelving to do, so once that was done there was nothing to stop you sitting at the desk and browsing through one of the back issues of Q Magazine or the other periodicals, that the library kept for up to a year after they were published. Aside from one regular, with a query about whether we had sheet music of some of Schubert's Lieder (*we did*), Glen and I pretty much had the place to ourselves.

7.30 arrived and after making sure all the visitors to the music library had left, I closed the till and brought it downstairs to the main desk and handed it in along with the total. Then I grabbed my coat and bag and we headed out the staff exit at the side of the building, hoping to catch the next number seven bus from Winston Square.

The library building was in the original part of the town, which dated back to its origins as a small fishing village before the fad for the restorative powers of fresh air and salt water had transformed it, like so many other places on the coast, into a resort, and a sizeable town had grown up to accommodate this new industry. Though most of the traces of the town's heritage from this period had long since been bulldozed, there remained a small but picturesque pedestrian area, near the library, which contained what was left of those narrow streets and houses, now transformed into shops selling handmade gifts, overpriced jewellery or novelties such as local rock and the occasional saucy postcard. I just happened to glance across the road as we walked by and that's when I saw her turning into the narrow warren of streets.

Claire.

I ran across the road but by the time I had, she'd already disappeared from view. Ignoring Glen's shouts from behind me, I headed in the direction I imagined she must have gone but my progress was slowed considerably by the fact that the old lanes made it impossible to get past if two people were walking side-by-side in front of you. After about fifty yards the passage opened up into a small square and there I thought I caught another glimpse of her, as she turned into another small side street.

"Claire!" I shouted, but she'd already passed out of sight again. An old lady to my left, gave me a curious look. I made my way across the square to the street she'd turned into but there was no sign of her. I looked left and right, trying to decide which was the most likely direction that she could have gone in. In the end, I turned left, which took me down towards the seafront.

I came out of the side street and narrowly avoided being hit by a teenager on a Vespa. I stepped back out of the way in time, but as I did so I lost my footing and fell backwards onto the pavement and landed on my backside.

"You alright, son?" asked a middle-aged man in an old-fashioned suit.

"Yeah, just lost my footing, that's all…"

"You want to be more careful crossing the road, all these bloody mods racing up and down the streets on their little scooters, you'll get run over if you don't have your wits about you."

"Yeah, you're right, I'm sorry…"

"Don't need to be 'sorry', son, just be safe - you'll live longer that way."

I nodded in agreement and he went on his way. I looked around to see if I could see any further glimpse of Claire, but it was no use. She'd clearly gone the other way.

That's when I noticed the street itself.

Something seemed very strange about it, but I couldn't put my finger on it. There were plenty of streets in town that seemed as if they'd been preserved in aspic for the last 30 years or so, but somehow this one seemed even more run down than normal. The colours of the houses, the shop fronts, all seemed completely out of date. There was a butcher's shop across the street, with slices of meat presented in the window. *That's a throwback to the old days*, I thought. Most of the independent butchers had shut down by now, with the majority of people preferring to buy their meat in the supermarket. I crossed over the road to look in the window, more out of curiosity than anything else. When I looked up at my reflection in the butcher's shop window, however, I looked completely different. My hair was shorter and I was wearing a polo shirt and chinos, instead of the Nike sweatshirt and stone washed jeans I'd been wearing that day. As I tried to comprehend this change in my appearance, a younger man walked behind me wearing a bowler hat. I turned and stared at him. *Who on earth still wears a bowler hat, anymore?*

"You alright there, sonny jim?"

I turned to find a uniformed policeman standing next to me.

"Erm...yes, thank you, officer, I just felt a bit dizzy that's all."

" 'ad a bit of a funny turn, whilst 'aving a look in the window of the butcher's, did we? I should cut along home, now, if I were you, lad. Don't you want you passing out in the street, now, do we?"

I just nodded, at a loss for words.

"Well, go then - hop it!"

I crossed back over the road and almost collided with Glen.

"Rob what the fuck is wrong with you? Why the hell did you just run off again like that?"

"I thought I saw Claire…"

"She's missing Rob, it's not like she's just going to be wandering around town!"

"I know, but it was her…I could have sworn it was."

"Look, it's just shock because you're worried about her, that's all. C'mon, let's get moving or we'll miss our bus otherwise."

As we turned and walked back up the way we'd come, I couldn't resist a glance back over my shoulder to see if the policeman was still watching me.

He wasn't.

He was gone and so was the butcher's.

Now it had become a health food shop.

III: BOYS DON'T CRY

Glen seemed to have forgotten all about my strange behaviour the next day. After school, we went back to his house, so that we could rehearse our set a couple of times before his dad dropped us down to the venue. We set up our gear in the living room as usual. I had left my guitar, amp and synth at Glen's after our gig the weekend before last, so that made things a little easier.

Although we'd already been at St. John's for 2 years by that point, we'd really only become aware of each other's existence after being thrown together on a French exchange trip. The two girls who we'd been paired with were best friends and spent virtually every waking hour together, often leaving Glen and I to chat amongst ourselves, whilst they conversed in French so rapidly that it was impossible for either of us to keep up with the conversation. Instead, we'd bonded over our mutual love of music, finding that we liked a lot of the same stuff: Wham's first album, The Eurythmics, New Order, Depeche Mode, Kate Bush, The Cure and, of course, Bowie. He didn't even make fun of the fact that the first single I'd ever bought was Bucks Fizz's *The Land Of Make Believe*. There were some bands we couldn't agree on, of course: Glen didn't really get my interest in Peter Gabriel and couldn't stand The Police (he hated Sting's voice and did a wickedly cruel impression of it, singing the chorus of *Roxanne* as if he had a hacking cough) and I never could get as enthusiastic about either ABBA or West End musicals. He also introduced me to a lot of stuff: Roxy Music, Gary Numan (both of which his older brother, Frank, had loved), Soft Cell (I'd heard *Tainted Love*, which became the first song we ever tried to do a cover version of, but not much else by them), Prince (who I instantly loved, even if reading the lyrics - some of which Glen had to explain to me - elicited the odd juvenile snigger) and Madonna, whose songs I didn't like that much, initially. *Get Into The Groove* was the first track of hers that I really loved. Glen bought the 12-inch single version and we just put it on again and again, dancing around to it in his bedroom, until eventually his parents shouted up the stairs and told us to "*please play something else!*".

The third or the fourth time that we played it, we were dancing quite close to each other and he leaned in and kissed me on the cheek. I stopped dancing and looked at him for a moment, then I moved in closer and kissed him on the lips. I don't know why I'd expected a boy's lips to feel different from a girl's - lips are just lips after all - but somehow I'd thought it would be different.

"What was that?" he asked, as we broke apart again a few seconds later.

"Not sure," I replied, shaking my head. "Don't get too used to it."

"It wasn't that memorable," he said, smirking.

Glen never actually told me he was gay. It was just sort of clear, at least to me. I envied his certainty. I didn't like boys (aside from Glen) and was definitely more attracted to girls, not that such a distinction mattered to the likes of Ollie Harding - *Glen was clearly gay, I hung out with Glen, therefore I must be gay too.*

Glen had gone for an HIV test a month before. To go for the test was nerve-wracking enough, but he was also worried that, as the age of consent for gay men was 21, admitting he was gay and sexually active might lead to questions from the police. Fortunately, the clinic didn't ask and his test was negative, but he told me how nervous he'd been waiting for the results. I knew exactly what he meant. Stories about AIDS were everywhere you looked and the public information films with their slogan of *Don't Die Of Ignorance* were shown virtually every advert break. It seemed only a matter of time before you found out that someone you knew had contracted it. Recently I'd started having a recurring nightmare. I was walking through a large hospital ward, the sun streaming in through the windows and the beds filled with young men turned prematurely old by the disease destroying their immune system. Glen was in the last bed on the left. He looked up at me as I approached the bed and stretched out a frail hand in welcome. That's when I would wake up in a cold sweat.

Later on, Glen would tease me about that kiss, asking if he was my first.

He wasn't.

My first proper kiss had happened the year before.

My mum often rented out the spare bedroom to visiting foreign language students coming to study English during the summer. Some liked it so much they came back again the next year. One of them, an 18 year old from West Germany, had introduced me to Pink Floyd by lending me her cassette of *The Wall* (highly ironic now I think about it, considering Germany's divided status at the time). The following year she brought me a copy of *Dark Side Of The Moon* on vinyl as a present. She also asked me to teach her all the English swear words - which, of course, I was only too happy to do. She repaid me by teaching me how to kiss and letting me practice on her. I'm sure that, for an 18 year old, kissing a 12 year old is about as sexy as kissing one of your cousins, but it meant a great deal to me at the time.

It was around the time of that first kiss with Glen that he and I had first started to get serious about making music together. I had taken guitar lessons when I'd first started at St.John's, but it had been classical guitar and the teacher had refused to teach us chords. After about a year I'd not progressed much beyond learning the notes on the various strings and playing a fairly ropey rendition of *Jingle Bells*. Frustrated, I bought myself a book of guitar chords with my pocket money and taught myself. Helpfully, the chord book had been arranged in such a way that along with each new chord it also showed you the other chords from the same key that would work alongside it, so you got an idea of what chords might go together, without needing to delve into music theory. I would spend hours moving from one chord to another and back again, until I could find the shapes with my eyes closed. I only really learnt the major and minor chords, plus a few of the sevenths, but at the time that seemed like all I really needed and it was certainly more than just the three chords all the punk musicians said you needed to know in order to be able to form a band.

Encouraged by my dedication, my Mum finally caved in and helped me buy a second hand Ibanez electric guitar and a tiny practice amp (which I eventually traded in towards a second hand Roland Jazz Chorus, with built in chorus, reverb and distortion - the same amp used by Andy Summers, Robert Smith and Johnny Marr - once I started to earn money working on Saturdays) and this is what I took with me to Glen's house when we rehearsed.

Glen's older brother had the synthesizer and sequencer sections from the Roland System 100 Modular system (which must have cost quite a bit when he bought it) and Frank very generously let Glen use it, occasionally. Having the sequencer module meant that Glen could record a rhythmic idea or a bass line and then play something else over the top. The System 100 was only monophonic, so you had to be careful you didn't play two notes at the same time, but it had two oscillators so splitting them up and sequencing one for bass meant there was another for lead lines. It certainly worked well enough until Glen eventually saved up enough money to buy his own synth: a Casio CZ101, as well as a Boss Dr Rhythm drum machine.

Even though it only had a small sized keyboard, the CZ101 was at least polyphonic and digital - meaning it stayed in tune and had patch memories, so Glen no longer had to take a minute between songs to set up the next sound. I was also substantially cheaper than the most ubiquitous digital synth of the day: The Yamaha DX7, which practically every band on Top Of The Pops seemed to own. One of the music teachers at St. John's actually had a DX7 and was kind enough to let Glen have a go on it. Glen told me that he personally thought the CZ101 sounded better, as well as being a lot smaller and lighter - an important thing to consider when you either had to rely on a lift from Glen's dad or a taxi to get you to a gig.

Of course, what we both really wanted was an Emulator II, the sampling keyboard that Chris Lowe from the Pet Shop Boys played whenever they did a tv appearance. New Order had one too and so did Depeche Mode. We'd had a big laugh the previous year when we'd seen *Ferris Bueller's Day Off* and he'd used samples of coughing and sneezing when he phoned up his school to tell them he was ill. Needless to say it was ridiculously expensive (even though it was less than half the price of the other famous sampling keyboard of the time - The Fairlight CMI) and no self respecting bank, not even T.S.B - *the bank that likes to say: yes!* according to their regular adverts, narrated by *The Singing Detective* himself, Michael Gambon - was going to lend that sort of money to a pair of students with part-time jobs. In our case it'd be more likely to be *the bank that likes to say: fuck off!*

That first rehearsal we attempted a few cover versions and then Glen told me he'd written a song and asked if we could try playing it. He showed me the chords and after a couple of times through, it was sounding pretty good, but what I was really impressed with was his lyrics and his voice. He'd been in the choir at school and could really sing. He even encouraged me to do backing vocals on the chorus, which I wasn't sure about at first - I'm not much of a singer - but the combination of our two voices together sounded nice.

Once we'd run through the song a few times, we recorded it on his portable cassette deck, which had a little microphone built in. The microphone compressed the mix together terribly and Glen had to practically stand next to the tape deck, so that his vocals would be heard clearly (we didn't have any microphones back then), but it had...*something*. It was certainly better than you might expect from two thirteen year olds making music together for the first time.

Over the next few months Glen wrote more songs. Some were good, others less so, but over time his average of good songs began to improve. After six months, we felt we had enough decent ones to go into a local recording studio, offering bands a special deal of a flat fee of £30 for 2 hours recording time. The studio would mix down what you had done in that time on to a cassette for you at the end and this was how the majority of local bands made their first recordings. We took the three best tracks and made a little cassette e.p. from them, taking them round to local music venues. Within a month we got our first gig, supporting another band and we made up a bunch of copies of the cassette e.p., with a cover drawn by me, to sell for a few quid. We were popular enough to be asked back the following month. In between, we found another venue that would let us play. Some of the bands we supported were kind enough to suggest us for other gigs and by the end of the year, we'd established ourselves enough that we could count on doing at least one gig, virtually every month.

I'd managed to find a second hand Roland SH101 synth by that time too, so we took Glen's Casio and drum machine, plus my little Roland, my guitar and my amp with us when we gigged. I mostly just used the Roland for the occasional lead or bass line, in addition to the main keyboard part played by Glen. I wasn't much of a keyboard player but as it was monophonic, like Fred's System 100, so even if I had been Richard Clayderman, I'd still only have been able to play one note at a time. One advantage was that it had a little arpeggiator built in, as well as a little sequencer which could store a bunch of notes which we used a couple of times during our set. It could only store one of these sequences at a time though - meaning we generally did one song that used the sequencer at the beginning of the set and one later on, which I meant I then needed to re-program the sequence during the break between a song, necessitating an extra long *"chat with the audience"* from Glen whilst I was doing so.

We ran through the setlist we planned to do that evening a couple of times and agreed on a cover of *Blue Monday* for an encore. We had enough songs by now that we didn't need to do covers but we occasionally did either *Blue Monday*, *Tainted Love* or *Love Comes Quickly* as a bit of fun at the end of a set. We played it through twice, with Glen deliberately singing one of the lines wrong to wind me up. The first couple of times that I had heard the song I had genuinely thought that the line after *"I see a ship in the harbour"* was *"I scan a shallow bay"*, rather than *"I can and shall obey"* which is what Barney Sumner actually sings - cue a fair amount of piss-taking from Glen the first time we tried to cover it and him habitually calling the song *"Blooming day"*, in mocking reference to my original mondegreen. Once we were done, we packed up all the gear into Glen's dad's Sierra and he dropped us down to the club.

P*ow!* was located in a couple of the old arches that ran underneath the seafront promenade. There was a short ramp up to the promenade next to the club, but no parking, so Glen's dad dropped us off at the curb, we unloaded the gear onto the pavement and then carried it down the ramp.

As we were the support act, we couldn't start our sound check until the headliners had finished theirs, so we put our gear just inside the entrance and went over to the bar whilst The Rayguns were on stage running through their setlist. The bar was on your left as you came in and the stage was against the back wall. The owners had painted the walls black and there were no windows so it was a little like entering a long underground tunnel, with its low rounded ceiling. The unmistakable stench of salt water was always present just as it was in every other building on the seafront. It was as if the salt had impregnated the very molecular structure of the metal and wood. You could clean the floors and walls as often as you wanted, the smell would always be there.

Glen and I both ordered a coke and the manager came over to say *"hello"* briefly, as we watched The Rayguns run through two more songs. They were one of the bigger local bands, who'd actually released their own album the year before and everyone thought were destined to get signed by a label sooner or later as their songs were really good with great lyrics and their lead singer, Julie, had a fantastic voice. They also always drew a good crowd too, which was why we were really happy to be supporting them.

They finished their last song and came over and chatted to us briefly whilst we were putting our gear on the stage. We ran through a couple of our tracks to a smattering of applause from a few of The Rayguns and the bar staff, before swapping out a duff cable on the right output of Glen's Casio and asking the engineer if he could make Glen's vocal a little bit louder in my monitor. We gave the manager a box of cassettes of our e.p. to sell by the entrance and then went across the road to the Wimpy Bar in Pearl Street to grab ourselves some dinner.

Sitting there, eating our cheeseburgers, we talked about who might turn up to see us play.

"Paul said he was going to come along and Jessica and Laura from my French class said they wanted to come. What about you?"

"Mark Davis said he might."

"Who's he?"

"He's in my computer class, his brother Rory plays violin in the orchestra."

"Yeah, ok, I know who you mean. Hey, and let's not forget: your favourite policewoman's also coming."

"Give it a rest, Glen...."

"Do we need to put her on the guest list or does she just show her badge and get in free?"

Shaking my head in exasperation, I happened to look out of the window towards the cinema across the road. Glen and I had been there three weeks ago to see *The Lost Boys*, which Glen had spent most of drooling over Kiefer Sutherland. It was still showing, along with *Dirty Dancing* and *Robocop*, which I really wanted to see. There were a bunch of teenagers milling about outside, either waiting for friends or cueing up to buy tickets and that's when I saw him.

The boy who'd been watching us in the woods.

He was there along with a bunch of other boys about the same age, but he wasn't looking at them, he was looking directly at us.

"Here," I said, giving Glen a fiver, "pay for me, there's someone I need to talk to…"

"What? Where the hell are you going, now?"

"I'll be back in a minute..." I grabbed my coat and rushed out the door. I could see the boy was turning away now and walking away from the others. I crossed the road quickly and quickened my pace in an effort to catch up with him. He turned into one of the narrow little alleys that go behind the houses on Pearl Street that are there for the residents to put their bins out on rubbish collection day. I reached the alley just in time to see him duck out of sight, as the alley bent around to the left slightly.

"Hey, come back here, I want to talk to you!"

I broke into a run and as I came around the bend in the alley I saw him up ahead once more. He had opened one of the doors that led from the alley into the backyard of one of the houses and had stopped there. He had his back to me and seemed to be looking up at one of the windows in the house. As I caught up with him, I naturally glanced up to see what he was looking at.

There, at one of the first floor windows was Claire. There was no doubt about it. She was wearing the exact same clothes she'd worn the previous Friday. She put her hand up to the window pane. I could see her lips move, she was trying to say something that I couldn't hear. Then the boy turned around towards me.

I screamed.

He had no face.

Where his face should have been was just a swirling mass of flesh, with no features at all. Where his mouth should have been suddenly tore itself open like a piece of wet dough and what sounded like a wounded animal's cry emerged from it. He came towards me. Stumbling backwards, I lost my footing and crashed back against the brick wall behind me. I brought my hands up to protect myself. As I closed my eyes and tried to turn my face towards the brickwork, I could feel the hot breath of his toothless, yawning maw on my cheek.

Then I felt the hand on my shoulder and screamed again.

"Rob? Are you ok? What's the matter?"

I opened my eyes to find Glen kneeling in front of me in the yard. The boy was gone and there was no Claire at the window either. Just me and Glen in someone's empty backyard.

I burst into tears.

"What the fuck is happening to me, Glen?"

Mercifully, Glen didn't start asking me questions about what had just happened, he just helped me to my feet and we walked back to the club. By the time we got there I'd recovered my composure a little. Which was a good thing because D.S. Morell was already waiting for us outside.

"Hi Rob," she said, as we approached. She stuck out her hand for Glen to shake. "Hi, Anne Morell, you must be Glen."

"That's right. Rob's told me all about you."

"Only good things, I hope."

Unable to stand these fake pleasantries a moment longer, I suggested we go inside.

Morell had wisely swapped her smart suit jacket and skirt for jeans and a t-shirt and fitted in just fine with the few other punters already beginning to file in. She stood at the bar and chatted with Glen and myself until it was time for us to get ready. It was all small talk, mostly asking about school or how the band was going. At no point did she mention either Claire or what was going on with the case. Anyone bothering to eavesdrop would have probably assumed she was my older sister.

Once we got on stage, she joined the throng of people near the front and swayed along happily as we launched into our first song and cheered and applauded like everyone else when it was over. I did my best not to look at her whilst we were playing, but found myself catching her eye between songs whenever I happened to glance in her direction. She was smiling and genuinely looked like she was enjoying the gig. I found myself remembering Claire and that gig at *The Jack and Jill*. Just like that night, it felt like I was playing for just one person.

Then, almost as soon as it had begun, our 20 minute opening set was over. The audience demanded an encore and *Blue Monday* went down a storm. I caught Glen's eye as I started the drum machine. He looked pleased, I hope I did too. It had been a really great gig.

We needed to clear our stuff off the stage as soon as we were finished, whilst the sound engineer made sure everything was set up properly for The Rayguns, but once we were done, we joined Morell at the bar once more.

"That was great, you were great...I'm really glad I got to see you play, " she said with what seemed like genuine enthusiasm.

"Thanks," was all I could think to reply.

"It was great you could make it," said Glen, who grabbed a drink and went over to chat to two girls I vaguely recognised from school.

"I don't think your friend likes me very much," Morell said, as soon as he was out of earshot.

"I think he's just a little curious as to what you're doing here."

"It seems as if it's more than that."

"More suspicious than curious, then."

"Was he suspicious of Claire too? A bit jealous, maybe?"

"No. He has good reason to be suspicious of you, though. I mean, do you often turn up at the gigs of people you suspect of doing something wrong?"

"No, but then you're not a suspect, are you Rob? Claire's simply gone missing...unless you know something I don't?"

"I'm not in the mood for this tonight, I'm afraid," I said, picking up my glass and starting to move away. Morell reached out and touched my arm. There was no force there, only a gesture to stop me from moving away.

"You can't hide from the truth forever, Rob. Sooner or later, you're going to need someone you can talk to about all this."

"About what?"

"Seen anything strange lately?"

I looked at her.

"Strange in what way?"

"Stuff that doesn't seem to make any sense. Things that can't be real, because otherwise there must be something wrong with reality."

"I don't know what you're talking about." I lied.

She leaned in closer and I felt slightly ashamed as I felt her body brush against mine as she did so.

"I understand why you're doing this…I'm probably the only one who ever really could." She touched my face gently and turned it slightly so that I was looking directly at her. "This can't go on for much longer. I can give you a little bit more time, but only a little." She smiled at me, but it was a sad smile. Like that of a parent who knows their child has done something wrong but wants to hear their side of the story. She let go of my face and squeezed my arm gently. "Go hang out with Glen and your fans, I'm sure they're dying to tell you how great you were this evening."

With that, she turned back to the bar and ordered another drink whilst I walked over to where Glen was, still baffled at what I'd just heard.

Glen and I stood and chatted to the two girls, who turned out to be the two from his French class that he'd mentioned earlier, until The Rayguns took to the stage. We watched the first 15 minutes of their set and then decided that we should probably carry our gear back up to the promenade and see if we could find a taxi. Jessica and Laura didn't live that far from Glen and agreed to split the cost of the taxi with us if we'd drop them home as well. Between the four of us we could carry all our equipment up to the promenade in one go. It was dark now and the breeze coming off of the seafront meant the temperature had dropped considerably. Even, so when I heard Ollie Harding's voice, a chill ran down my spine.

"I see you pair of bum boys finally found some girls then..."

Glen said something to Jessica, who immediately put down the bag of cables she was carrying and went back inside the club. I didn't hear what he said and I didn't need to. *He'd told her to go back inside and get Morell.*

"Oh dear, did I scare one of the fag hags away?" Ollie was about halfway up the ramp to the promenade, blocking our way to the road.

"Grow up, Ollie you pathetic little wanker!" Laura shouted at him and went to move past him but he pushed her back. "Don't you push me!" she shouted, but Glen put a hand on her arm.

"All by yourself, Ollie?" I asked, "Where are the rest of the Hitler Youth tonight? Washing their hair?"

Glen glanced across at me with a look that practically screamed *Shut the fuck up now, Rob!* but I wasn't deterred and neither was Ollie. He and I took a step towards each other. I heard a small click and there was the flick knife in his hand. Even with everything else going through my mind I still had time to wonder where on earth he could have gotten his hands on one - they'd been illegal for years.

I heard the door of the club open and a blast of the Rayguns set for a few seconds, before it was muted once more. I hoped that meant that Jessica had managed to find Morell and she wasn't just standing there by herself.

"Really, Ollie? A knife?" I heard a gasp from behind me, probably Jessica who couldn't see what Ollie had in his hand. "Not even you're insane enough to try and actually use it - you'd go to prison."

"Borstal - I'm under 18, remember?"

"It'd still follow you around for the rest of your life. Every time you tried to get a job. Am I really worth all that hassle?"

He moved a little closer and brought the knife up to my chin. I tilted my head back slightly, in response to this. I couldn't help it.

"Not so cocky now, are you, poofter?"

"Why Ollie?"

"Why what?"

"Why am I worth ruining your life for?"

"Maybe I just want to wipe that stupid smile off your face..."

"Then do it, if that's what'll make you happy."

"Rob, please...don't." I heard Glen say.

"You should listen to your little boyfriend, there. He knows I'll do it, even if you don't."

I leant in towards the knife and let it graze my cheek, slightly.

"No you won't. If you'd wanted to stab me you'd have already done so. You could have got me in the back when we came out of the club. I wouldn't have even seen you coming. This is about trying to scare me, but it's not working out the way you planned, is it?"

I could see from his eyes that I was right. He hadn't expected the 4 of us. He'd thought it would just be Glen and I, or maybe that I'd be on my own. Yet something in his personality, some fault in his code, had meant that even though it wasn't how he'd imagined it, he'd gone ahead regardless.

"Put the knife away Ollie and go. It's the only option you've got left."

"The woman standing over there is a Police Officer, Ollie." I saw Ollie's gaze flick across first to Glen and then briefly to Morell. "If you so much as scratch Rob with that knife of yours, you'll be arrested on the spot." I saw the shake in the hand holding the knife. The look in his eyes had changed.

"Detective Sergeant Morell, South East Constabulary, Ollie. Put down the knife and give yourself up. Don't make things any worse."

Ollie kept looking at me, the knife still near to my face. He took a couple of steps backwards shaking his head and turned and ran. Morell pushed past us and ran after him. I turned back towards Glen and Laura. Glen was almost crying. He marched over to where I was and slapped me in the face.

"What the fuck were you thinking? Didn't I tell you he was a psycho? Why the hell would you provoke him like that? He could have killed you!"

"He wasn't going to stab me in front of D.S. Morell..."

"Fat lot of good she did you! She didn't even mention that she was a copper until I said something. She just stood there watching!"

Much as I didn't want to admit it - Glen was right: Morell had done nothing to stop Ollie. It was as if she'd been waiting to see whether or not I could handle it by myself.

IV. GAMES WITHOUT FRONTIERS

Quite how the news about our showdown with Ollie Harding got around as fast as it did, I'm not sure. The only logical explanation would be Laura and Jessica telling all of their friends as soon as they got to school the following day, because by the end of the first lesson, when I saw Glen in the cafeteria, the entire school seemed to know about it and it was the first thing he told me when I sat down next to him.

The second thing he told me was that Ollie hadn't shown up to school today.

"Have you heard anything from D.S. Morell?" he asked.

I shook my head. She'd not been able to catch up with Ollie after he'd run off and had come back to where we were waiting for a taxi, still shaken by what had happened, a few minutes later. She'd told me that I would need to make a statement about what had happened, but it could wait until the following day and in the meantime we should all go home and she would go back to the station and file a report.

"Maybe you should call her?" Glen suggested, "I doubt she'll be surprised that Ollie's not in school today but you should probably let her know all the same."

I agreed to call her from the registry phone, afterwards. "Are you ok?" I asked him.

He looked at me for a few seconds. "No, I'm not sure I am. I keep thinking about how calm you were when Ollie was pointing the knife at you and how strange you've been acting lately."

"It's been a pretty strange week…"

"That's the understatement of the year, Rob."

There wasn't much else I could do but agree.

I went to the registry, just along the corridor from Felton's office on the first floor landing. It was double the size of a class room and, when you walked in, there was a counter with at least two secretaries working there. The day's registers would be handed in every morning and behind the secretaries stood rows of shelves containing the records for each student. At the far end of the counter was a pay phone, with a phone book attached to it via a piece of thick string. The secretaries glanced up as I walked in the door but then went back to their work, when I moved over to the phone. I couldn't find Morell's card anywhere in my pockets or bag, so I looked up the number for the local police station in the phone book and dialled the number. As soon as someone answered I deposited my 20p into the phone.

"Hello, can you put me through to D.S. Morell if she's available, please?"

"Who?"

"Detective Sergeant Morell…M.O.R.E.LL.."

"There's nobody here with that name."

"I beg your pardon?"

"There's no Detective Sergeant Morell stationed here, sir, you must have the wrong number."

"This is South East Constabulary headquarters, isn't it?"

"Yes, sir, but I'm afraid there is no Detective Sergeant here with that name."

I hung up the phone. There was a strange feeling in the pit of my stomach.

I turned around and saw that both the secretaries had gone.

I was alone.

I pushed open the door to the registry. The only sound I could hear was the creak of the door's hinges.

Directly across the hallway was the teacher's lounge. I went over to the door and knocked. Normally, you could hear a smattering of conversation from behind the door before one of the teachers came and opened the door to ask what you wanted, but I couldn't hear anything at all. I pushed open the door gently, expecting to be reprimanded by one of the teachers inside, but there wasn't anyone in there either. A cigarette lay smoking in one of the ashtrays by the window. Next to one of the chairs was a still steaming cup of tea.

I headed back to the cafeteria. Not 10 minutes ago, when I'd been talking to Glen, it had been almost full. Now, it was completely deserted. I walked through the cafeteria and out the other entrance to where there were some classrooms, these were all empty too. Books still lay open the on desks, bags lay on the floor next to the chairs, but there were no students and no teachers.

Except me.

I walked along the silent corridors and headed to the toilets to splash some water on my face. I turned the tap on full and closed my eyes for a few seconds. It was only when the mirrors in front of the basins began to steam up that I realised that I must have turned on the hot tap by mistake. I turned off the tap and went to open the window to let the steam dissipate. Then I glanced at the mirror and saw what had been written there in the condensation:

GO HOME

I ran home through the empty streets. When I reached my front door I found it was unlocked.

"Hello?" I called out as I stepped inside. "Is anyone there?"

Silence.

Morell appeared at the top of the stairs.

"Come on up, Rob, it's time you and I had a proper chat."

I went upstairs and found Morell sitting in my room, on the edge of my bed. At least I hadn't left any underwear lying around.

"Where's my Mum? What happened to all the people?"

"Calm down, Rob, your Mum's fine. This is just a glitch in the matrix."

"What?"

"It's just a saying…come and sit down, I'm not going to hurt you."

I didn't move. "Who are you? I know you're not a police officer."

"I know. That's why I thought it was the right moment to have a chat - just the two of us."

"What are you talking about? Where did everybody go?"

"I'll explain everything if you let me. I needed a way to get close to you and to make sure things were moving in the right direction after Claire's disappearance. Pretending to be the police officer investigating what had happened seemed like the most obvious way."

"Taking a bit of a chance weren't you? What would have happened if a real police officer had turned up asking questions - or was it the case that she was never really missing in the first place?"

Morell smiled. "That's one way of looking at it, certainly."

I removed the rucksack from my back and threw it across the room at her. "No more riddles!," I shouted. "Tell me what happened to Claire!"

"Take it easy, Rob."

"Don't tell me to take it easy! Tell me what the hell is going on!"

"Claire disappeared because her character had fulfilled its function."

"What are you talking about?"

"Claire wasn't real. None of this is real."

"You're insane…"

Morell walked over to the bookshelf and picked up my copy of Stephen King's *'Salem's Lot*. It was the first of his books that I'd read and I'd re-read it several times since. She opened it up at one of the first pages and handed it to me.

The page was blank.

All the pages were blank.

She picked up another book from the shelf at random. It was completely blank too.

"Check as many as you want," she said. "They're all blank because your memory can't remember the text accurately."

"This is some kind of trick…"

"It's not. Can you name any of the songs you and Glen wrote? Can you remember any of the lyrics?"

"Of course. There's…" I stopped. I couldn't remember the name of a single song, let alone any of the lyrics.

"You know how, when you're in a dream everything seems to make sense, but when you wake up you realise none of it did?"

"Are you telling me this all a dream?"

"More like a nightmare that you can't wake up from; one that, if you don't escape from it soon, won't let you wake up at all."

"I don't understand."

"In here, you're 17 years old having the time of your life, but in reality your body is slowly dying, whilst your mind is attached to a fantasy world."

"What do you mean '*in here*'? What is this supposed to be? A simulation? Am I inside a computer program like in *Tron*?"

"Think about it, Rob. Think of all the strange things that have happened over the last few days. Is that really so hard to believe? What other explanation is there that everybody could just disappear like that?"

"It's impossible, no computer could manage it - the amount of data that would require would be astronomical."

"In 1987, yes. But this isn't really 1987 and you're not 17 - you were never 17 in 1987. If you don't believe me take a look at the photo on the bookshelf over there."

I picked up the photo in the glass frame. It was a good quality black and white print of a photo that had appeared in the local newspaper when footballer Sir Bobby Charlton had come to visit my junior school. He'd given a whole bunch of the lads who were football fans (which included me at the time) a special coaching session. At the end, a bunch of us had posed for a photo alongside Sir Bobby, proudly holding up a towel that we'd each been given as a memento. I was on the extreme right of the photo directly next to the man himself, in a football shirt and shorts.

It had been years since I'd looked at it and my Mum had given up all hope of trying to dust in my room - she had enough of a job creating a path through to the window in order to draw the curtains. As my thumb wiped away the thick film of grey topsoil that coated the frame, I gasped and dropped the picture. Fortunately, the thick carpet meant that the glass didn't break. The picture landed face down, with a slightly muffled thump. Morell bent down and picked it up.

"Now, do you see?" she asked, turning over the frame and pointing at the younger version of me in the photo.

I did.

The young boy staring back at me from that black and white image was a few years younger, the date scrawled on the bottom of the photo was June 1985, but the resemblance was clear.

He was the boy with no face.

Except now he had a face.

My face.

"This is the boy I keep seeing…"

"That's the part of your brain that still remembers that you were 11 in 1987, not 17. It's trying to tell you something isn't right. Maybe it's time you started to listen to it."

"But if this is all taking place inside my head, how come you're here? Or are you also just another manifestation of my brain?"

"No, I'm real. Though obviously I'm not really here. What you're seeing isn't really me anymore than the version of you is really you. This is just an avatar - a digital representation of me, though this is more or less what I look like. I'm connected to your mind through the computer system that's running all this. In the real world we're sitting next to each other."

"And why you?"

"They figured I knew you better than anybody else and if anyone could persuade you to leave, it would be me."

"They?"

"Your co-workers. The company you own."

"I *own* a company?"

"A big one. Developing software and games for computers." She held out her hand to me. "Come back with me and you can see for yourself."

I took her hand and went back downstairs with her. The younger me was waiting by the front door.

"He'll take you to the exit," Morell said, "but you have to choose to leave. He can't force you and neither can I."

I nodded.

"And be careful. I don't quite know what's going to happen when the simulation realises you want to leave it behind."

"Why should it mind, it's just a computer program?"

"It needs your mind to survive. If you leave, it won't exist anymore. Just be careful and remember - *none of this is real.*"

It was starting to get dark when my younger self and I left the house, which logically would make no sense as it had only been about 11 am when I'd returned home, but I'd long since stopped worrying about what was logical and what wasn't. We cut through the deserted streets in silence until we reached the street where Claire lived.

I stopped and looked across at the house. It was dark just like all the others that we'd passed on the way. The younger me tugged at my hand, impatient to get going again, but I shook him off.

"There's something I want to see," I told him.

I walked on and turned the corner into the next street. There, I found the narrow alley that separated the back gardens of the two streets, where the owners would place their rubbish bins for collection.

Fortunately, some of the houses had printed the house numbers on these doors as well, making it easier to figure out which door led to which house without needing to keep count. I traced my way back until I found the wooden door that led to the back garden of Claire's house. The door was locked but, guessing that it was probably only secured by a single bolt, I aimed a hefty kick at where I imagined the lock might be. On my second try the lock splintered away from the wooden frame and the door swung open.

The younger me put his hand out to stop me from entering and shook his head. I pushed him out of the way and entered the back garden.

There were steps leading down from the kitchen and up from Claire's basement room to the modest-sized patio garden, which I remembered Claire's mum had lovingly planted with flowers in the borders and a small selection of vegetables, such as runner beans and tomatoes running along the far wall - all gone now. I made my way over to the steps leading to the basement. It was a typical back door, wooden with a few glass panels in its centre. It was locked. I tried kicking at the door but it didn't even budge. I remembered seeing a key in the lock on one of the times I'd visited Claire and tried breaking one of the glass panels with my elbow to no avail; then, after searching around the garden for a bit, I found a decent sized stone and used it to break one of the glass panels, reach through and unlock the door from the inside.

The room was completely empty and smelt the way rooms do when they've been that way a long time. There was a thick layer of dust on the floor.

It was as if the house had been deserted for years.

"See? There's no one here," my younger self, who was waiting by the door, said. "Let's go. We shouldn't be here."

Satisfied that I couldn't have logically been here less than a week ago, I turned to leave, but as I did so I heard a noise from the far end of the room. I looked back and peered into the gloom.

"Rob?" a voice called from out of the shadows, "Is that you?"

It was definitely Claire's voice but there was something strange about its timbre. I could just about make out a figure curled up on the floor in the far corner by the window. As I moved closer, I saw it was Claire, with a sheet wrapped around her.

"Claire, what are you doing here?"

"Waiting for you. Where have you been? I've been waiting for you for ages…"

As she tilted her head up to me, the moonlight through the window illuminated her face.

I stumbled backwards in shock and horror.

Her eyes were bloodshot black, her face white, her lips blue and around her neck, a ring of livid purple-yellow bruises that retained the impression of whatever thin piece of material had been used to garrotte her.

"Don't leave me again, Rob…" she gargled from her lifeless mouth. I realised then why her voice had sounded strange before, it was the voice of something with a crushed windpipe that somehow still had the powers of speech.

She reached out towards me and the sheet fell away. She was completely naked, scratches and bruises covered her pale form. I backed away from her towards the centre of the room.

"Where are you going?" said another voice from beside me in the darkness.

I turned as Glen shuffled into the patch of moonlight, but it wasn't Glen as I knew him. His eyes were black too and his face was pale and full of sores. He'd lost much of his hair and what was left of his body was clothed in a hospital gown that hung on his frame, like a sheet on a washing line.

"No," I mumbled, backing away from the pair of them, "this isn't real..."

"How's this for real?"

I was aware of someone rushing towards me out of the darkness. I caught a glimpse of the glinting blade just before it was buried deep in my gut. I screamed once and then again as the knife was wrenched from my stomach and thrust in once more, slightly higher up. I looked up to see a black-eyed Ollie grinning at me.

"Told you I'd kill you, didn't I, you fucking little ponce?"

I grabbed the hand that still held the knife sticking into my abdomen. It hurt more than anything I could possibly describe, but I wasn't about to let him pull out the knife and stab me with it again. He tried to tug his hand free, but I held fast.

"You're not real, none of you are..."

"Keep telling yourself that when your guts spill out all over the floor!" Ollie replied with a twist of the knife. I screamed again. Claire and Glen were clawing at me as well. The shock and the blood loss were making me feel weak. I could feel myself beginning to drift away.

"Just saying it isn't enough," I heard my younger self shout. "You have to make yourself believe that it isn't real!"

With my last ounce of strength, I focused once more and grabbed Ollie's wrist even tighter, looking him squarely in the eye.

"You're not real," I repeated. "The knife isn't real either." Even as I said this, the pain lessened. I looked down once more at his hand that I was gripping so tightly. There was no longer a knife in it. I smiled. "You're nothing to be afraid of." I brought my free hand up to his forehead and prodded him, sharply, between the eyes with my index finger.

He popped like a balloon, spattering bits of himself all over the room and the ceiling.

I wrenched myself free of Claire and Glen and ran towards the door, still clutching my stomach, even though it was completely unharmed. My younger self grabbed my hand and pulled me through the door, before slamming it behind me to stop the ghastly versions of Claire and Glen from escaping. I went to help him, but he pushed me away and leaned his back against the bulging door.

"Go!" he shouted. "I can't hold them for much longer!"

"I don't know where I'm supposed to go!"

"Yes, you do. Part of you has always wanted to leave. Where do you go, when you feel that way?"

Claire's hands came through the broken pane of glass, grabbed my younger self by the throat and began to choke him. I tried to pry her hands loose, but it was no use. I could see his eyes start to close. I turned and ran out of the garden, back into the alley behind the houses.

It was no longer empty.

It was filled with people standing shoulder to shoulder. Mario and the rest of Ollie's gang, Mr Felton, Mr Tiller, Laura and Jessica - half the town, it seemed. All with lifeless black eyes, staring at me, waiting. Behind me I heard the crash as Claire and Glen finally managed to break out of the door to the basement.

It was now or never.

I charged towards the nearest end of the alley, with my head down, trying to break through the crowd of dead faces. I succeeded in knocking a few of them out of the way but then I felt their hands grabbing at me, tugging at my clothes and trying to hold me back. I disappeared under a sea of grasping bodies but continued to try and inch my way to the end of the alley on my hands and knees. Through the melee of legs and feet I could see the end of the alley now and clawed my way towards it as if trying to emerge from a rugby scrum. Eventually, my hands found the corner of the brickwork and I managed to pulled myself clear and get to my feet.

I didn't need to stop and look back. I could already hear them coming after me.

I took the same route that I'd taken two nights previously, cutting through the side streets towards the railway viaduct. These were all deserted too. I reached the viaduct and crossed over the road to where the small door was. As I did so, I saw another crowd of people massing on the far side of the viaduct. I looked behind me and saw the other group that had now almost caught up. The two crowds began to advance towards me, steadily closing in. I tried to pull myself up on the brickwork next to the door, but slipped and fell back down with a bump.

They were getting closer.

I pulled myself up on the brickwork again and managed to get a handhold on the grass bank this time, but then I felt myself start to slide down once more. Just as I thought I was going to lose my grip entirely and fall back into the waiting arms of Claire and the others, a hand reached out and grabbed mine.

"Come on, Alice, time to leave Wonderland."

Morell reached down and helped pull me up on to the bank, just as the first of the crowd reached the door. We raced up the steps to the top of the viaduct. Behind us I could hear the splintering of wood as the door was broken down. We moved carefully on to the tracks, avoiding the lines themselves. About 200 yards away I could see a goods train moving slowly out of the station on the middle track.

"That's our ticket out of here," Morell said, "we need to climb on board it, just like you always dreamed of doing."

"Rob, please don't leave us!" I heard a voice behind me shout. I turned and saw Claire and the others had now also reached the tracks. She now looked just as she had done the previous Friday. Glen looked normal again too. He was holding Claire's hand, there were tears in his eyes.

"If you go, we won't exist anymore," he said.

Morell gripped my hand. "They didn't exist in the first place. You made them up, like a character in a book - don't listen to them, come back to what's real."

"What we had *was* real," Claire pleaded: "We can make it go back to just how it was - you have the power to do that, Rob. You can make this world whatever you want it to be…we can be together, all three of us."

"Don't listen to them! They're trying to keep you here, because they need your mind to survive. They're feeding on you like a parasite."

The train was almost next to us, now, Morell moved closer and got ready to pull herself up on to the handrail and steps leading to the driver's cab.

"Rob, please, it's now or never…"

Claire was stepping across the tracks towards me.

"Don't leave…"

"Rob, come on!"

Glen holding his hand out towards me.

"Dad! *Please*!"

Claire and Glen stopped. I turned and looked at Morell. I wondered for a moment whether I'd misheard her. Then in that moment it all came back to me and I recognised her for who she really was.

My daughter.

She held out her hand to me and I grabbed it and pulled myself up onto the train.

"I'm sorry…" was all I could think to say. Whether I was saying it to Claire and Glen or to Anne, I wasn't completely sure. The train began to pick up speed. I saw Claire and the others just standing there on the tracks now, watching. I felt the edges of my vision began to close in. It was as if I was heading into a long tunnel. Eventually, all that was left was darkness.

V. SYSTEM ADDICT

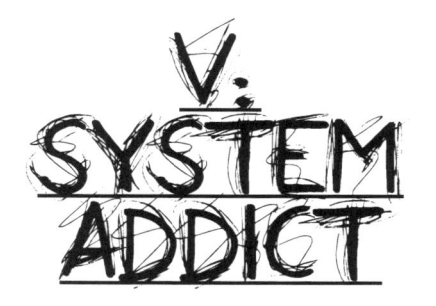

I think that just about wraps things up. Thank you for going through your account once again for me. I'd like to go through a series of cognitive control questions.

Ok.

What is your full name?

Robert Mark Langley.

What year is this?

2044.

How old are you?

67.

Are you married?

Not anymore. Widowed. Two years ago.

Children?

A daughter, Anne.

What do you do for a living?

I'm the C.E.O. of a software company.

What is Teenage Wildlife?

pause.

Please answer, Mr Langley…

A simulated A.I. environment, based on my home town in the year 1987.

Very good.

I woke up in a hospital bed, with Anne at my side. She looked just the same as she had before, just with more modern clothes.

"Hi Dad, are you ok? How are you feeling?"

"Thirsty," I croaked.

She gave me some water, through a straw, from a beaker on my bedside table. The cold water felt soothing, but it hurt to swallow.

"How long?" I managed to ask her eventually.

"About 2 days. You were conscious at first when I brought you out, but you collapsed soon afterwards and I had you brought here. The doctors think it was probably just a combination of exhaustion and dehydration, but they're going to run some more tests to make sure."

"Make sure of what?"

"That you didn't irreparably damage either your body or your mind whilst you were off pretending to be a teenager again."

I could see the tears welling up in her eyes.

"That bad, huh?"

She nodded.

"Hey, there's no need to cry. It's ok. I'm still here. You saved me. Who's my brave girl?"

"I am," she said, wiping away the tears.

There were plenty of tests over the next few days. Physically. I wasn't too bad, considering I'd been essentially living in my head for almost a week, with just an IV drip for nourishment. It wasn't my body the doctors were worried about, however. As soon as I was well enough. I was given an exercise book and a pen and told to write down, in as much detail as I could remember, my experience of being inside the simulation in preparation for my sessions with Doctor Alison Williams, who was responsible for assessing my mental state.

Do you suffer from depression?

I've never been diagnosed.

But you do get depressed?

Sometimes, yes. Why?

Certain aspects of your life inside the simulation: your apathy towards your hometown, your dislike of your school and teachers, the regular bullying. Were you actually bullied as a teenager?

Yes.

Was it as homophobic as it was in the simulation?

Sometimes. Though it had very little to do with whether you were actually gay or not. Back then, homophobia, like sexism and racism, was far more overt than it is now. We were used to it. It's only when you look back at old tv shows and sitcoms that you realise just how normalised we were to it all.

Surely in the South East, where you were from, people were a little more tolerant than other parts of the country?

It was and it wasn't. There was a large, openly gay community, particularly in and around the arts scene, but that didn't stop people being homophobic. This was just one year before Thatcher's government introduced Section 28. A large percentage of the South East was, and still is, filled with white, middle class, Tory voters - who are generally fairly intolerant of everything.

Did it make you depressed?

Which? The bullying or living in my hometown?

Both.

Well, I did daydream about leaving and going somewhere else. But I think part of that is also geographical. If you're born right next to the sea, then you really only have two directions you can go: abroad or inland and I think that fundamentally changes your view of the world. As for the bullying, that just made me angry.

Does it still make you angry, when you think back about it?

Of course, you don't forget that sort of thing.

It doesn't sound like a moment in your past you'd be happy to go back to. Why chose to set the simulation then?

Choice has nothing to do with it. In order for the simulation to really feel real, it needs to be a time and a place you have actual memories of. The reason why there had to be a bully like Ollie Harding is because if there wasn't, it wouldn't have seemed real. I wasn't one of the cool kids at school, I was an outsider. Always the last one to be picked for teams in sport, nobody's secret crush and definitely not a rebel. I was an average student, mostly trying to keep my head down and out of trouble, staying clear of anyone who seemed like they might have a problem with me - be it teachers or pupils. If I'd created a world where I wasn't those things, my brain would have rejected it immediately. Did you know that I originally tried to set the simulation in 1967?

Was that what happened when you were following Claire? You somehow fell back into the previous iteration of the simulation?

It seems that way. Although, so far, no one's actually been able figure out how that could happen. Anyway, the reason that first iteration didn't work was because it was no different from every other virtual reality environment that has been created over the years - There's no real connection, you just feel like a tourist. Eventually, I realised that the reason why I couldn't really connect with it properly was because I had no real world experience of my hometown, at that time. I would have had the same problem if I'd set the simulation somewhere else in 1987. I know what it was like to be alive in my hometown in that year. I had actual memories of it that could be bolstered and enhanced by archival information and anecdotal evidence. As I'm sure you know, Doctor, our memories are not fixed but permanently in a state of flux. If you reconnect with a copy of something from your past, a song, a book, a film, a photograph - then your past memory of that thing will be updated by this new information. So, for instance, if you asked me to picture, in my mind's eye, a 1987 edition of *Smash Hits* magazine, then the result will probably be fairly vague. However, put a copy of *Smash Hits* from 1987 in my hands or even a scan of one and I will immediately start to generate a whole bunch of memories of the magazine from that year: which bands had been interviewed, who'd been on the cover, even down to a mental image of the eleven year old me, standing in the newsagents about to buy it. Those memories will then be added to my existing memories creating new neural pathways and solidifying into a concrete experience of me buying that exact magazine in 1987.

Was the simulation a form of therapy, then? Changing aspects of your past in a way that you weren't able to in reality - dating the girl you had a crush on or standing up to a bully?

That definitely wasn't my primary reason for creating it, but I guess you could look at that way.

So what was the main motivation behind it then?

Isn't it obvious? To see if it could be done.

To make a virtual world indistinguishable from actual reality?

At least whilst you're inside it - yes.

So why that particular year?

I believe that a great deal of our personality becomes fixed at some point in early adolescence. It may well vary based on gender and experience but somewhere around 1987, when I was 11 years old, was when it happened to me. A lot of things happened that year: I moved to secondary school, I started to notice girls and that was also the time when I started to become really passionate about music - I would regularly watch *Top Of The Pops* and *The Album Chart Show*. I cared about bands releasing new singles and where they were in the Top 40 chart. I was fascinated by every aspect of music: the lyrics, the videos, haircuts and even the brands of instruments people played, but my age meant that I had no chance of going to see any bands play, least of all at clubs such as Pow! I dearly wished I could be a little bit older, just like Tom Hanks in *Big*. I was also a late bloomer and Kylie Minogue would have been taller than me back then. I wished I was older and taller, could go to gigs and maybe even have had a chance with the cute sixth former, who used to come and help me with my Maths homework.

This was the girl who was the template for Claire?

She's an amalgamation of quite a few different women, including my late wife, but yes, she was one of the templates.

What aspects did you take from her for Claire?

Mostly her appearance, but she did also work in a clothes shop in the town centre.

Did you go and visit her where she worked, like you did in the simulation?

Yes.

It sounds as if you were slightly obsessed with her.

I was certainly infatuated with her.

It sounds like more than just an infatuation. Do you often still think about her?

Not really.

Does that mean 'not often' or 'not at all'?

It means I haven't forgotten her, and will be unlikely to, as she was probably the first person I ever fell in love with. Surely, you remember the first person you ever fell in love with, Doctor?

Of course. But I'd like to think that'd stop short of trying to re-create them in software form. Who was the template for Glen?

A boy I used to sit next to in Science class, plus another boy I later played in a band with.

Did you ever tell either of them that you found them attractive?

No. I'm not even sure if they were both gay.

So, like the template for Claire then, Glen is really just a fantasy. The gay best friend and confidant for a teenager unsure of his own sexuality?

The whole thing is a fantasy, Doctor. None of these people are real, they're just constructs.

Perhaps you'd care to explain that, please. For the record.

Just as it is essential to ground the world of the simulation in reality - using a real location that you have some experience of, in the period when you're setting the simulation - it's equally important *not* to base the avatars within on any one particular person from your past.

So, all the characters are in fact hybrid creations? You didn't have a headmaster who you nicknamed "One Up", for instance?

No.

So why is it important not to base the avatars on one particular person from your actual past?

Again, it comes back to how you interact with the A.I. within the simulation. If you based it on a real person and then the A.I. made them react in a way that might seem completely justifiable within the context of the simulation, but which you, with your knowledge of the real person, knew their real life counterpart would never do, then that would alert you to the fact that the world of the simulation wasn't real.

Surely, given enough information about the real person, the A.I. could convincingly plot what the most realistic reaction would be?

Hypothetically, perhaps…but in fact the human brain is incredibly sophisticated in spotting little errors in behaviour, often more so than we realise. Even with a massive amount of data about a person, the A.I. could still conceivably make small errors in the reactions that would be enough for the user to know something wasn't right. Have you ever read the interview transcript with the LaMDA A.I. at Google?

Yes.

Can you remember what you thought when you read the transcript extracts? Was there anything in there when you read that tipped you off to the fact, just reading the interview text itself, that it wasn't a human being who was being interviewed?

It was a long time ago, so I can't remember exactly, but yes, there was definitely something odd about the A.I.'s responses.

I had the same reaction. There was something about its use of language that always bothered me. I couldn't put my finger on what it was at first, only that the conversation seemed a little stilted. Eventually after studying the transcript for some time, I realised that the A.I. never hesitates or shows reluctance.

Why would it?

Exactly, but that's also what betrays its synthetic nature. Its answers often began with "Yes, of course…" or "I'd love that…" What human being would answer so readily and positively to every request made of it? If I asked you, as the interviewer does in the LaMDA transcript, to come up with a very short children's story with some sort of inherent message, you would be reluctant. You would certainly need time to consider what the story would be and you might even need to stop and start again whilst you were telling it. LaMDA never does and that was enough to suggest to some small part of my brain, the part leftover from some more primitive state of evolution perhaps, that something wasn't right. It wasn't just about what it said, it was *how* it said it.

Do you believe LaMDA was actually sentient?

I'm not totally convinced, no, but I guess that depends on your idea of sentience, doesn't it?

Surely, most would agree it's about self awareness of existence?

Yes, but at what level? You could certainly make an argument that a cat or a dog is aware of its existence, but not, perhaps, in the way you and I are. It's difficult to say for sure because we really don't have any idea how non-human brains work…in fact, we have enough trouble figuring out how the human ones work, most of the time. Anyway, that's not really the point I'm trying to make, here. It's not about whether LaMDA is actually sentient, only that our brains are sophisticated enough to tell the difference between a human response and an artificial one and that's why the avatars in the simulation need to be hybrid constructs.

What about your worries about contracting AIDS within the simulation? Were they genuine or just something you felt you needed to add for the sake of historical accuracy?

No, that was a genuine fear that the eleven year old me had. Public awareness of AIDS grew exponentially throughout 1987, because by then heterosexuals were also being diagnosed with it. There were even cases of people contracting HIV through blood transfusions. A massive public awareness campaign was launched, with public information films, a leaflet delivered to every home in the country and countless news stories and coverage about it.

But you were only 11, at the time. Why would that make you so afraid at that age?

I know, it's ridiculous when I look back on it now, but it's true. I would change the channel whenever those films came on, especially the one with the guy waiting for his test results. The irony is that, watching them as an adult, the films themselves are really quite innocuous - not a patch on the public safety films about what to do in the event of a nuclear attack or those telling kids not to play near pylons or railway tracks from a few years earlier. Yet somehow, none of them had the effect on me that these did. Perhaps because they were intrinsically connected with sex, which I'd only just become aware of…anyway, it felt as if it was so prevalent that my generation were almost bound to get it. It's not quite the same, but when Anne was about 11, the first wave of Covid hit and everyone had to go into lockdown. I remember how frightened she became listening to the news every night. It was the same with me. Suddenly, there's this thing that it seems anyone can catch with potentially fatal consequences.

I must have dozed off again.

When I woke up, Anne was sitting next to the bed again wearing different clothes.

"Dad? Are you awake?"

"Hmmm? Yeah…is everything ok?"

"Paul Stevens is here. Do you feel up to talking to him?"

"Paul?"

"Hey there, chief. How's my favourite client?"

"This hotel sucks. The food's not great and the room service is terrible."

"Good to know that your sense of humour's still intact."

"If they've sent you, then it'll probably need to be. Have the board fired me yet?"

"You know they're not going to do that - they can't. Nobody's looking to blame you for what you did. They might make a strong recommendation that you take some time off - paid, of course. They're understandably concerned, shall we say, at their C.E.O. working on a secret side project like Tony Stark, but they won't stay like that for long. Even the most unimaginative accountant among them realises that you've possibly just cracked open the next frontier in digital technology. A virtual world, almost indistinguishable from reality, are you kidding me? They think all their Christmases just came at once!

"This isn't The Sims, Paul," Anne replied. "This is more like the virtual reality version of Jurassic Park. It almost killed him. If I hadn't altered the simulation's code, it would have done. If they try to shoehorn this technology into a product just so they can make a profit, they're going to have a million lawsuits on their hands."

"Calm down, Anne. Nobody's talking about releasing any part of this as is. All the board want to know is: has he damaged himself so badly that someone else needs to take over, or will he be able come back, once he's fully recovered, and turn this into the most successful intellectual property the company has ever created?"

"How can you even think about asking him to come back? You're supposed to be his friend, as well as his lawyer?"

"Will the two of you please stop talking as if I'm not in the room?" I replied, silencing them both momentarily. "So what you're saying, Paul, is that this will be developed with or without me?"

"Rob, you know it will. They *have* to develop it. If they don't, someone else will."

"And yet, no one else has been able to do it the way he has," Anne replied.

"Because they didn't have Rob's genius."

"Genius, huh? That's what they're calling it these days, is it?"

I saw a thin smile creep across Paul's lips.

"You know what they say: Every idea is stupid, until it makes a ton of money. Then it's genius."

I laughed. Anne didn't.

So Anne altering the code was what caused the hallucinations?

Some of them. The simulation removed Claire, once her purpose had been fulfilled. Just as it did Ollie and presumably would have done to Glen, if I'd stayed there long enough, in a similar way to Conway's Game Of Life removing cells that have no living neighbours. However, Anne drawing attention to Claire's disappearance caused a dislocation between my brain and the A.I. and I think that's why I started to see glimpses of Claire or the younger version of me - it was my mind trying to tell me that something was wrong. When Anne then deleted all the other avatars in the simulation, the A.I. panicked and tried to reassert control over the simulation.

By re-instating the avatars and have them attack you?

Yes.

So, in other words, it began to fear for its existence?

That's one way of describing it…

How would you describe it then?

Its code was altered, causing inconsistencies in its programming.

These inconsistencies caused it to behave erratically?

Yes.

Behaviour that could be described as "fearful", could it not?

You're assigning it an emotion, when it's just really just a result of it not knowing how to respond to something not covered by its programming.

So you didn't program it to feel existential angst?

No. How could anyone possibly try and program something to feel that?

How do you explain its reaction then?

Look, this isn't *The Terminator* or H.A.L. in *2001*. This isn't *The Matrix* trying to crush humanity because it fears its own destruction. Our idea of what artificial intelligence will be like is more than 50 years old and it is as redundant as all our other visions of the future. A.I. has been in our lives for generations, already. It's in your shopping cart preferences, your music, book or tv recommendations and every single advert you see whilst searching the internet. It's sharpening your photos, adjusting your thermostat and setting your alarm clock. It doesn't try and kill you when you override its suggestion and sleep in longer. What A.I. is really good at is seeing a range of options and extrapolating information from them and you don't need that many parameters to create something complex. When it's connected to your brain with access to your own memories it will create variables and a range of responses based on your own responses. It's really no different from playing chess against a computer, which is also powered by A.I. by the way. Every decision you make, whether it's skipping class, doing your homework, asking out the girl, confronting a bully or forming a band leads to a narrow possible set of outcomes. A.I. then selects what it believes to be the most likely, based on your previous action, its previous responses, context etc. And because the reaction is contingent on the action that preceded it as well as the context, it's a lot more realistic than traditional multiple choice situations or standard programming. The same action could, in theory, elicit a different response in different situations, just as they do in real life. For example: you want to ask a girl out on a date within the simulation. If you choose to blurt out your question in front of her friends, or in the middle of French lesson, for example - then there's a better than average chance the A.I. will respond with her telling you to "*get lost*". However, if you instead chose to do it when you're alone together, perhaps when she's shown some interest in you or what you're doing - then the odds rise sharply in your favour. This isn't done by teaching the computer about an abstract concept, like human nature, it's simply letting it pick from a range of options where history and context are mitigating factors. Getting turned down by a girl because you used a corny pick up line doesn't require any more processing power than denying you access to a website if you keep entering the wrong password. What happened here was the same thing. It could sense something had changed in its operational parameters and it responded. That's not the birth of consciousness - it's the result of a series of limited options.

But its response was hostile. Hostility, by its very nature, suggests some form of self preservation instinct, surely?

No, you're assigning it emotions again. It just reacted, because the parameters, which it needed to continue to function, had changed.

Ok, but that's still self preservation - that's consciousness...

But viruses are capable of self preservation - is a virus conscious? No. You're adding two and two together and coming up with five.

What do you imagine would have happened if Anne hadn't guided you out and the agents of the A.I. had got hold of you?

I would guess that the simulation would have reset itself and everything would have started again.

Which means that it would have trapped your mind inside the simulation? Perhaps even Anne's as well, if she was still connected to it?

Possibly, yes.

And might it have then made it more difficult for you to leave, the next time?

It would certainly learn from whatever mistakes it felt it had made previously.

Then it sounds to me, like you had a very narrow escape indeed.

Perhaps.

Ok. Leaving that aside for a moment, now that we've gone through your account once more, do you now have some idea about what I might have found problematic about it?

Not really, no.

Really?

No.

You didn't begin your account at what most would consider to be the logical start point - your entry into this simulation that you created. Instead, you began it at the point where Claire went missing. At several points in your account, you look back on events that you couldn't have actually experienced - yours and Glen's history together, for example - as if they were things that had happened in your past. On top of that, by your own admission, you failed to recognise your own daughter, at first. We asked for a description of what your experience was like inside the simulation. What you've given us is a novella, where the narrator seems to have no more clue as to what's happening than the reader does. A fantasy version of you as a teenage pop star.

I was trying to be honest in my account.

What part of your account is honest, Mr Langley? I mean, I certainly feel I now know a lot more about the synthesisers of the 1980s or your favourite music from back then, but in terms of what events actually happened and which were simply manufactured memories, supplied for you by the A.I., even I'm not sure.

I meant being honest about my experience of what it felt like to be inside the simulation. Yes, I didn't recognise Anne at first and yes, whilst inside the simulation, those memories seemed real…

Which events did you actually experience? You were in the simulation for less than a week, very little of this could have happened in real time, there must have been moments where the time was compressed,
like when you went to sleep, for example.

Yes, obviously.

So which events did occur? Kissing Glen in his room would seem to be the earliest event, chronologically, that happened in some detail. Or did the simulation begin even earlier with the two of you meeting on the French Exchange trip?

I'm really not sure, I did meet a close friend of mine on a French Exchange trip - I can't be sure how much of that is now mixed in with my memories of meeting Glen.

Which is exactly why this is so troubling. If you'd simply created a fantasy world that had no relation to you or your own childhood then any signs of aphasia, for example, would be much easier to spot. Ok, let's assume that the memory of the Exchange trip is simply a fusion of your own childhood memory, with what you've created as background for the character of Glen. What might be the logical starting point for your time inside the simulation? Your first rehearsal together perhaps?

That I definitely remember happening in real time. I remember how many attempts it took to learn *Tainted Love* for example.

How many?

At least five before we could play it all the way through.

Ok, but the kiss occurred before the first rehearsal, so was that something you actually experienced or was that just backstory?

No, that felt real...*and* that's not based on something from my life, so it must have happened within the simulation.

Ok, that's good - now we're making progress - were you aware of a gap?

A gap?

A portion of time being missing.

No.

What would be the next detailed event that actually occurred? Running into Claire at the Jack and Jill?

Could be.

Nothing in between?

Not that I can think of.

What about you and Glen recording the demo tape?

It's there, but it's hazy and the memory of the recording studio could be based on my own life experience of recording in the same studio as a teenager.

So. The kiss, the first rehearsal, meeting Claire and, presumably, that Friday afternoon you spent with her before she goes missing. Aside from the events actually detailed in your account those are the only ones that we can be relatively sure, you actually experienced.

That sounds about right.

I'll be brutally honest with you, Mr Langley, I'm not sure it's possible to say for definite whether or not you've suffered any form cognitive damage yet. I think that will really only reveal itself in time. You may find yourself unable to distinguish your actual memories from those created by the simulation, you may find yourself mourning the avatars you've created as if they were actual friends that you've lost…I simply don't know. I'm not completely convinced, even now, that you're able to really separate fact from fiction.

Well, then ask me some questions. Let me show you that I can.

Very well. How do you know you actually left the simulation and this is actually reality?

What possible reason would the simulation have in trying to fool me like that?

To make you believe that you'd escaped it, when in fact you're still in there.

That's assigning it a sentience that it doesn't possess, at least as far as I'm concerned. It doesn't have the programming to do that either.

It's connected to your brain. It knows what you know. It feels you start to resist it, it senses you want to leave. It responds by making it more difficult for you to do so. In the end, it decides its best option would be to trick you into thinking that you left. By your own admission, its programming was changed when Anne altered the code, so you have no idea how it's currently functioning. Its modes of operation may have completely changed, because of that. Could it not have evolved enough, after almost a week of being connected to your brain to do that? To be able to mimic a scenario where you think you've woken up, when in fact you're still inside? Think about how many people have you really interacted with here, a handful at best. The simulation has access to memories involving your daughter and your lawyer, so it could easily re-create them as avatars. Everyone else, myself included, could just be like the other avatars from your home town - loosely based on someone you know or knew.

So who are you based on?

A doctor who once treated you, perhaps…I could be a combination of any number of people. When we met, did you have the sense that we might have met somewhere before?

No.

Are you sure?

Yes. I'm sure I'd remember someone as attractive and interesting as yourself.

That's a cute line, but it doesn't prove anything. After all, wouldn't the simulation design me that way so that you'd let your guard down? Aren't I your perfect idea of a young female doctor? One that you'd find sympathetic and attractive? What about if I undo my top button, like this, so you can see more of my cleavage when I lean forward, to ask a question? Would that make you more willing to talk to me?

You're forgetting something. If I didn't make it out of the simulation, then Anne would be trapped there too.

How do you know she isn't? Equally, how do you know that this version of Anne isn't just part of the simulation? A double bluff. An avatar claiming she's your daughter, that tells you you're inside a simulation and then she is here to help you leave, when it fact it's just the simulation fooling you once more.

I'd know the difference.

Because of how sensitive your brain would be to any errors in the simulation?

Exactly.

But you didn't even recognise her at first, your own daughter...why did she call herself "Morell", by the way?

If this is all still the simulation, then you already know the answer to that.

Humour me.

It's her mother's maiden name. She's always used it professionally, because she wanted be accepted on her own terms.

Would you say the two of you are close?

Yes. We always were. Even when she was younger. I practically raised her. I was the one working from home, programming.

But she doesn't live with you anymore.

Of course not, she's a grown up and she's a busy woman.

So you don't see each other that often?

We do…when we can find the time.

Is she married?

No.

Is she in a relationship?

She was. A long term one, but they broke up a while back.

Do you know why?

The guy was a prick.

You didn't like him?

I thought she could do better.

That must have caused some friction between the two of you.

A little, yes.

And yet, she's the one who comes to rescue you. Out of all the people, including those at your company, who you would think would have a better knowledge of whatever software the simulation was running - she is the one chosen to step inside the simulation and try and bring you out...does that sound plausible to you?

She's a brilliant programmer in her own right and she knows me better than anyone. She would be the logical choice in that situation.

She also seems very forgiving towards a father who has decided to lose himself in a teenage fantasy world. In my experience, daughters aren't generally sympathetic to their fathers pretending to be horny seventeen year olds. Doesn't she sound almost too good to be true? The brilliant daughter who can not only undo the mess her father has got himself into but, in the process, reconcile with him. Tell me that doesn't sound just a little bit like the fantasy of a father who has become estranged from the child he once felt so close to?

It does. But it also sounds like Anne and, if you knew her, you'd understand why she would come into the simulation after me - the little girl who could code almost before she could read and write, who designed a website when she was six, was creating her own simple computer games by the time she was seven and selling them on the App Store by the time she was ten. She wasn't just the only person who would be able to come into the simulation after me, she was the only one who could really appreciate what I'd managed to create…why are you smiling?

Because you're demonstrating how well you can differentiate between reality and the simulation. which is encouraging.

I'm glad to hear that. Your attempt to make me paranoid also had a fundamental flaw in its reasoning, though, Doctor.

Which was?

If Anne isn't real then she didn't actually alter the code of the simulation, so it's still operating under the original parameters that I gave it, so the simulation would have no need to panic and react the way it did or to try and fool me that I have escaped - that would be paradoxical. Therefore, Anne has to be real and because of that you and everyone else I've encountered since I've been here are also real. That's how I know I am no longer part of the simulation.

Very good. I had you going there for a moment though, didn't I?

If you say so. You can do your top button up again, now…

After a week, Doctor Williams was satisfied enough with my progress that I was discharged. The hospital gave me some crutches, as I was still a bit unsteady on my feet and because of this I agreed to stay at Anne's house at first, so she could keep an eye on me. I didn't mind. It had been a while since the two of us had so much time together.

One day she took me on a trip back to my home town, not that there was much left that I recognised anymore. It had been at least ten years since I'd last visited and the few remnants of my childhood that had previously still been standing were now gone. Winston Square had been completely redeveloped in the late 90's and then again in 2035. Now its homogenisation into a shopping mall that resembled every other shopping mall throughout the land was complete. Not that there were many actual shops left in it, of course. As with everywhere else, those that remain are simply storefront collection points for online retailers. The days of browsing through records, cds, books or even clothes, have long since been and gone. Anne and I amused ourselves a little at first, by trying to define exactly where things had stood in the simulation but eventually we had to stop, as it was making me depressed.

We tried to find where exactly *Pow!* had been but that also proved tricky, now that the entire seafront had been remodelled and much of what could have acted as a landmark for us to get our bearings were gone. The beach huts, the promenade and even parts of the beach itself, had been removed to make way for *A Seaside Experience,* renowned for its cleanliness, first class dining and family activities, trying as hard as possible to make you forget you were right next to the notoriously smelly and plastic-strewn English Channel.

On the way out of town, we drove around the streets where I'd lived as a teenager. Aside from the odd new housing development, it had remained more or less intact. We went past St. John's which also looked more or less the same. A few new buildings dotted around the school campus and a noticeably smaller playing field compared to my day, but otherwise it all still resembled the place I went to almost 50 years ago.

Anne parked the car and we walked in through the main entrance and looked around briefly. That part of the school was exactly the same and I was amused to find that smell of the building was exactly as I had remembered it in the simulation. Whatever else has changed in the last 50 years, the chemicals they use to clean school buildings are not amongst them.

We drove home and after dinner that evening I broached the subject of my returning to work and continuing my work on the *Teenage Wildlife* project.

"I'd only be advising, of course…trying to adapt the simulation into something they could market and I was thinking, maybe you wanted to come onboard as well? You know all the potential areas that we would have to look at in order to make it safe…"

"It's a nice idea, Dad, but no. And if I'm really honest with you, I don't think you should go back to it either. Let one of your team take over the running of it, or hand it over to the company completely even and just sit back and collect the royalties on it.

"You mean retire?"

"Why not?"

"But what would I do all day long?"

"Whatever you want. Buy yourself a vintage guitar and an Emulator II and write some songs, get ahold of an old computer and write programs in BASIC or just stay here and keep me company."

"You'd get bored of me pretty quick if I did that…"

"Maybe. But it's still better than the thought of you going back to work on *Teenage Wildlife*. The more you involve yourself in it, the harder it'll be not to go back into the simulation. You'll tell yourself that it's just to check on a few details and that it won't be the same this time and it's true - *it won't*. Next time, the simulation won't let you leave. You barely got away this time, even with my help. You won't be so lucky a second time. Please, Dad…for my sake, if not your own - *don't go back*. It'll kill you."

What else could I do but agree, even though I knew it was a lie?

Anne went to bed an hour ago. I've been sitting here in my room looking at my reflection in the mirror, ever since, trying to make peace with the man I see staring back at me.

The first time that I looked in the mirror, after I'd come out of the simulation, it was a shock. In fact, the doctors were so worried about the effect of me seeing a balding, paunchy, elderly man instead of the skinny seventeen year old with a mop of unruly hair, that they made sure that any mirrors or reflective surfaces in my room were covered.

But I know who I am now.

I can play for time a little. Have the company put someone else in charge of the project in the interim, but eventually I know that I will have to continue my work on *Teenage Wildlife*, because I want to go back inside the simulation.

Anne,

The reason I've kept on writing this account since leaving the hospital is because I want you to know that this is my choice. It wasn't Paul or the board who convinced me or twisted my arm.

Doctor Williams was right: part of me is still stuck inside it. Not because I can't distinguish between reality and fantasy, but because I prefer the fantasy. Part of me misses it - my version of the way things were back then. I miss Glen and I miss Claire and I'm sure I can fix things.

In there, I have so much. Out here, all I have now is you and no matter how much you love me, you can't spend the rest of your life looking after me - I won't let you. Unlike Bowie, I actually want to be a piece of Teenage Wildlife.

I hope you can forgive me.
Dad.

Acknowledgements

Despite having my name on the cover, books are rarely written alone and as usual I'm very grateful to those who helped me putting this book together.

My friend and proof reader, Stephen Ball, who has read each of my books and is always incredibly helpful and kind in his corrections and feedback.

Nick Langley at Third Kind Records, who not only read and made suggestions on the manuscript and but was also influential in working on the soundtrack album that I've created to accompany this book, as well as giving advice on the cover, layout and all the other aspects that go into getting a book ready for publication.

Finally, Mat Smith for his advice and assistance with the back cover blurb - something I always find tricky, but especially so in the case of this novel, where I had to be careful how much of the story I wanted to reveal.

Enjoyed the book?
Now listen to the soundtrack!

Rupert Lally's soundtrack to this book is now available as a digital and limited edition CD release via Third Kind Records.

Listen and buy it here:
https://thirdkindrecords.bandcamp.com/

also available:

Solid State Memories

What would you do if the person you loved most in the world was gone and no-one remembered them?

Dr Alex Wells wakes up to find her partner, Rachel, missing and her own nanotechnology implanted in her. Fleeing sinister government agents and unable to trust either her colleagues or her own memories, she must piece together what happened to her before it's too late.

In his debut novella, musician turned author Rupert Lally draws inspiration from the likes of J.G. Ballard and Philip K. Dick in a speculative sci-fi story about the nature of memory.

Rupert Lally's soundtrack to Solid State Memories is now also available on digital and limited edition vinyl from Third Kind Records

Listen and buy it here:
https://thirdkindrecords.bandcamp.com/album/solid-state-memories

also available:

BACKWATER

Separated by the past, connected by the future…

Teenagers Aife and Matthew live in different eras. After the deaths of their respective fathers, both of them begin journeys that will change both the future and the past, and lead them, inexorably, to each other.

Moving between the bronze age, the present and beyond, Backwater is an epic adventure through time to try and change the fate of the world.

Printed by Amazon Italia Logistica S.r.l.
Torrazza Piemonte (TO), Italy